Rowland Eyles Warburton

Hunting Songs

Sixth Edition

Rowland Eyles Warburton

Hunting Songs
Sixth Edition

ISBN/EAN: 9783744770583

Printed in Europe, USA, Canada, Australia, Japan

Cover: Foto ©Andreas Hilbeck / pixelio.de

More available books at **www.hansebooks.com**

HUNTING SONGS.

SIXTH EDITION.

HUNTING SONGS

BY

R. E. EGERTON WARBURTON

LONDON
BASIL MONTAGU PICKERING
196 PICCADILLY
1877

CONTENTS.

CONTENTS.

PAGE

viii CONTENTS.

INTRODUCTION.

 SHORT account of the Club for which fo many of them were written will not, I hope, be thought an inappropriate introduction to a new edition of thefe Hunting Songs.

The Tarporley Hunt was eſtabliſhed in the year 1762, and their firſt meeting was held on the 14th of November in that year. Hare-hunting was the ſport for which they then aſſembled. Thoſe who kept harriers brought out their packs in turn. If no member of the Society kept hounds, or if it were inconvenient to bring them, it is ordered by the 8th Rule that a "Pack be borrowed and kept at the expenſe of the Society."

Societies ſuch as the Cycle in Wales had in the earlier years of the laſt century been favourite meeting places for the Jacobite gentry; but whatever were the politics of the founders of Tarporley Club, it was evidently the love of hunting only that brought

*them together; and from that day to this, difference
of political opinion has never been known to interfere
with the election of the members, or to disturb the
harmony of the Club.*

*The Founders were the Rev. Obadiah Lane, of
Longton, county of Stafford, who had married
Sarah, sister of the first Lord Crewe; John Crewe,
son of the Rev. Joseph Crewe, Rector of Barthom-
ley and Astbury; Booth Grey, second son of Harry,
fourth Earl of Stamford; Sir Henry Mainwaring
of Over-Peover; George Wilbraham, the builder
of Delamere Lodge; his brother, Roger Wilbraham; Richard Walthall, second son of Peter
Walthall, of Wistaston; Robert Salusbury Cotton,
son of Sir Lynch Salusbury Cotton, of Combermere;
and the Rev. Edward Emily, whose connection with
the county I cannot trace.*

*The original rules recorded in the first club book
will not, after an interval of a hundred years, be
without interest to the modern sportsman, showing,
amongst other particulars, the hours which they
kept, and describing the dress in which our forefathers took the field:—*

> " *Tarporley Hunt, Nov. 14th, 1762.*
> *Mr. Lane, President.*
> *Mr. Booth Grey,* } *Secretaries.*
> *Mr. Crewe,*
> *Miss Townshend, Lady Patroness.*

" *We whofe names are hereunto fubfcribed, do agree to meet at Tarporley twice annually. The firft meeting to be held the fecond Monday in November, and the fecond to be fixed by the majority of the members who fhall meet at the firft ; each meeting to laft for the fpace of feven days.[1] We do likewife agree to fubmit to all the underwritten rules, and to all other fuch rules as fhall be thought necef-fary by the majority of the Society, for the better keeping up of the fame.*

Oba. Lane, Pres.	*Edward Emily.*
J. Crewe, Sec.	*Ric. Walthall.*
Booth Grey, Dep. Sec.	*R. E. Cotton.*
Henry Mainwaring.	*R. Wilbraham.*
George Wilbraham.	

" *1ft. Any member that abfents himfelf muft pay the fum of one guinea unlefs his excufe fhall be allowed of by the fitting members.*

" *2nd. Every member muft have a blue frock, with plain yellow metalled buttons, fcarlet velvet cape, and double-breafted fcarlet flannel waiftcoat, the coat fleeve to be cut and turned up.*

" *3rd. The harriers never to wait for any member after eight o'clock in the morning.*

---

[1] *The firft hunting day is meant by the fecond Monday. The Gentlemen having agreed to meet overnight.*

" 4*th*. *If the majority of the Hunt prefent are at home on the hour dinner is ordered, they are not expected to wait.*

" 5*th*. *Any members that fhall caufe or make any difturbance during the meeting (upon refufing to fubmit to the fentence paff'd on them by the majority of the Society) fhall be immediately expell'd.*

" 6*th*. *If the Society confifts of an equal number, the Prefident has a cafting vote.*

" 7*th*. *A new Prefident for the following meeting to be balloted for the laft day of the preceding meeting. The Prefident muft manage all the bufinefs of the Society during the time of his office.*

" 8*th*. *If no member of the Society keeps hounds, or if they do and it fhould be inconvenient for them to bring them, a pack muft be borrowed and kept at the expenfe of the Society.*

" 9*th*. *Three collar bumpers to be drank after dinner, and the fame after fupper; after they are drank every member may do as he pleafes in regard to drinking.*

" 10*th*. *The Prefident, as foon as elected, to nominate the Lady Patronefs for his meeting, fhe being a fpinfter.*

" 11*th*. *No member to be chofe but by Ballot, and none but the members prefent at the Balloting to have a vote : which Ballot muft be the firft night of the meeting.*

" 12th. The Houſe bill muſt be pay'd the ſeventh day of each meeting, and after that is done every member has the liberty of going after his own inventions.

" 13th. Every member has the liberty of introducing his Friend, but muſt pay for him as far as his ordinarys.

" 14th. All ſingle or private engagements muſt yield to the time fixed for the meeting of this Society.

" 15th. Should the members of this Society in a party attend any of the neighbouring aſſemblys, the Preſident muſt aſk the Lady Patroneſs for the time being, to dance, ſhould ſhe be there.   .

" 16th. If any member of this Society ſhould marry, he is to preſent the Hunt with a pair of ſtiff-topp'd well ſtitch'd buckſkin gloves each.[1]

" 17th. This Book muſt be kept in the Balloting box, and the Preſident for the time being muſt keep the key.

" 18th. The Preſident muſt acquaint Mr. Southon of the time appointed for each meeting.

" 19th. Every member that does not attend muſt ſend his reaſons in writing to the Preſident.

" 20th. Any member who advances the money for an abſentee, to be reimburſ'd by the Society in caſe of

---

[1] Pro buckſkin-gloves lege buckſkin-breeches.—BOOTH GREY, Dep. Sec.

ſuch abſentee's refuſing to pay him, and the abſentee to be expell'd.

"21ſt. *The Secretary muſt acquaint every member of their elections as ſoon as choſe.*

"22nd. *All forfeitures to be apply'd for the benefit of the Society attending the meeting when they are forfeited.*

"23rd. *The Preſident to forfeit five guineas for non-attendance unleſs his excuſe ſhall be allow'd of.*

"24th. *If any member abſents himſelf for a night during the meeting he ſhall forfeit one guinea for every ſuch night of abſence, unleſs he have leave of the majority of the Hunt preſent.*

"*The orders of the Tarporley Hunt, November ye 14th, 1762.*

"*Ordered, that Mr. Booth Grey procures for the uſe of this Society a Balloting-box, with eighteen black and eighteen white balls.—O. Lane, Pres.*

"*Ordered, That Mr. Booth Grey procures for this Society two Collar Glaſſes, and two Admittance Glaſſes of a larger ſize.—O. Lane, Pres.*

"*Mem^m.—An Expreſs was ſent this meeting to Cheſter for a Chine of Mutton by Obadiah Lane, Clerck.*

"*Ordered, that Mr. Coton have the thanks of the Society for a ſet of Silver Bottle Tickets.*"

The remainder of this book contains the proceed-
ings of the firſt forty-ſix meetings, the account of
ſubſcriptions, and the liſt of forfeits down to Feb.,
1785. The extraɛts I ſeleɛt will ſuffice to give the
reader an inſight into the manners and cuſtoms of
that date, and will ſhow likewiſe how completely
Foxhunting, when once introduced, ſuperſeded the
ſport for which the Club had been originally founded.

" 1763.—Nov. ye 6th. Voted, that the metal
Buttons be changed for baſket mohair ones. Voted
that after ſupper but one collar glaſs is obliged to be
drunk. Voted, that every member provides himſelf
a ſcarlet ſaddle cloth, bound with blue.

" 1764.—Feb. ye 6th. Voted, that each Preſident
provides two dozen Franks during his meeting for the
uſe of the Society. Voted, that each member, when
he marries, inſtead of providing Breeches for every
member of the Hunt, does pay into the hands of the
Secretary for the uſe of each member, the ſum of
one guinea to be ſpent in leather breeches.

" Nov. 5. Voted, that the number of members of
this Hunt be limited to twenty. Voted, that if any
member does not appear in the ſtriɛt uniform of this
Hunt, he ſhall forfeit one guinea for every ſuch
offence, viz., a plain blue frock, with cuff turn'd
up one button, with mohair buttons, and unbound ;
and ſcarlet velvet cape, with a double-breaſted

ſcarlet waiſtcoat, a ſcarlet ſaddlecloth bound ſingly with blue, and the front of the bridle lapt with ſcarlet.

"1765.—*Nov.* 4th. *Mr. John Barry having ſent the Fox Hounds to a different place to what was ordered, and not meeting them himſelf at that place, was ſent to Coventry, but return'd upon giving ſix bottles of Claret to the Hunt.*

" 1766.—*Feb.* 3. *Voted, that any member of this Hunt that marries a ſecond time ſhall give two pairs of leather breeches to each member of the Hunt. Five guineas out of the forfeits given to the poor.*

"1766.—*Nov.* 2. *Mr. Crewe fined for having his bridle lapt with red and blue. Mr. John Barry fined for not having taken the binding off the button holes of his waiſtcoat. Mr. Whitworth fined for having his ſaddlecloth bound with purple. Lord Groſvenor fined for riding to cover with a white ſaddlecloth, and likewiſe for having his bridle lapt with white. Lord Groſvenor having quitted the Hunt on the Tueſday without leave, was fined five guineas.*

"1767.—*Nov.* ye 1ſt. *Mr. Arthur Barry received the thanks of this Society for Heber's Horſe Racing from the year* 1751 *to* 1766. *Voted that for the future they ſhall be taken in annually.*

"1768.—*Oct.* ye 30th. *Parliament meeting ſooner*

than common this meeting by the confent of majority was held a week fooner than appointed by Rule.

" *A. Barry pays one guinea for a waiftcoat with improper pockets.*

" *Lord Grofvenor appearing two days out of uniform, both coat and waiftcoat, pays for each day 2 guineas, and one guinea for abfenting himfelf one night without leave.*

" *Books belonging to the Hunt, Nov. 13th, 1768 :—*

> *17 Volumes of Heber complete.*
> *Annual Regifter complete.*
> *Pocket Library.*
> *Oxford Magazine.*
> *Howard's Thoughts.*
> *Oxford Saufage.*
> *Hunting book.*

" *1769.—Nov. ye 5th. Agreed, that the number of this Hunt fhall be enlarged to twenty-five members, but fhall never exceed the fame. Agreed, that the Rule*[1] *fhall be altered, and that inftead of three collar glaffes only one fhall be drunk after dinner, except a fox is kill'd above ground, and then, after the Lady Patronefs, another collar glafs fhall be drunk to Foxhunting.*

" *1770.—Voted, that the Club in general do not*

---

[1] *Rule* 9.

c

dine out by invitation. Voted that the Hunt change their uniform to a red coat unbound with a fmall frock fleeve, a green velvet cape, and green waift- coat, and that the fleeve has no buttons: in every other form to be like the old uniform, and that the red faddle cloth be bound with green inftead of blue, and the fronts of the bridles remain the fame as at prefent. The buttons bafket, fame colour as the coat, waift- coat buttons colour of waiftcoat. Every one not ap- pearing as above liable to the old forfeitures.

" Nov. 4th.—Riding a hack to cover or a fhooting or upon an accident happening, or horfe on tryal, not to be fined according to the ftrictnefs of rule made in regard to uniforms.

" 1772.—Nov. 1ft. During this meeting (on the 5th of November) the Lord Prefident was pleafed to fignify his intention of invefting Thomas Chol- mondeley, Efq., of Vale Royal, in this county, with the moft noble order of the Belt. Accordingly he was introduced to the Lord Prefident by two fenior alder- men. The Whip of State was borne by the Secre- tary: the Belt, carried on a cufhion of ftate, by the Mafter of the Foxhounds; Sir Thomas's train was borne by the junior members and the Prefident's by the Coverer. Great attention was paid during the ceremony, every member ftanding, and Sir Thomas, returning to the chair, his health was drunk with three cheers. Ordered, that he always

*appear in the enfigns of his order during the meeting.
Voted, that any perfon who fhall be hereafter eleɛted
a member of this Hunt, and is a married man, fhall
pay £10. 0s. 6d. on his admiffion by way of Stock-
purfe, and if a Bachelor fix guineas. Inftead of
Breeches, twenty guineas voted to be paid.*

"*As* [1] *Mr. Prefident has done this Hunt the honor
of his Piɛture, their thanks are return'd for the
fame.*

"*Lord Kilmorey's mild and pleafant adminiftra-
tion was approv'd, not only by his fecond eleɛtion,
but by his health being drunk in three Gobblets.*

"*1773.—Nov. 7. Voted, that every member in-
troduɛng a ftranger pays for the 2d night of his ftaying one gallon of Clarett; for the 4th night of his
ftaying 2 gallons; and if he ftays three Hunting
days, one dozen. Voted unanimoufly, that Mr.
John Barry is defired to fitt for his piɛture for this
Hunt. Mr. John Barry very politely confents.*

"*1774.—Feb. 6th. Lord Kilmorey by his own
defire is no longer a member, but voted a letter to be
wrote to him that it is the wifh of the London
Hunt that if he is in Town he will try the Bond-ft.
covers as a member.*

"*Nov. .—Wilkinfon ordered to take back the
great chair, and either to alter it to the approbation*

---

[1] *Lord Kilmorey was Prefident. There is no record of this
portrait having been in poffeffion of the Club.*

of the Hunt, or to make a new one, charging nothing for the same; on this condition the gentlemen agreed to pay him for the great chair.

" *This meeting Sir Thomas Broughton paid forfeit to Booth Grey for a match to have been run.*

" 1775.—*Nov. This meeting a sweepstakes was won by Sir Thomas Broughton starting against Mr. Crewe, of Crewe. Lord Stamford, Geo. Wilbraham, and Lord Kilmorey paid forfeit.*

" 1777.—*Feb. Ordered, that a cover, or covers on the Forest be made from the Stockpurse, under the direction of Sir Peter Warburton, George Wilbraham, and Mr. Peter Heron, if leave can be obtained.*

" *November. Ordered, that the ropes for Crabtree Green are paid for by the President, £5 17s. 0d. Ordered, that Mr. Grey is paid for the repairs of the course, £5 19s. 0d. Ordered, that Mr. Wilbraham is paid for sowing and inclosing a cover, £16 0s. 0d.*

" 1778.— *February. Voted, that Mr. Wilbraham gives Mr. Stevens as a compliment for drawing the lease of a cover on the Forest the sum of five guineas.*

" *November. Voted, that an order made the eighth meeting, Feb., 1776, that the part of that order containing these words, 'that the Claret never be admitted into the house bill' shall be rescinded, and that the* aeficiency of the Claret, after what is pay'd for ſtrangers, &c., be inſerted in the bill.

"The Secretary's accounts were ſettled and allow'd, being on the Claret account £15 5s. 6d., and on the houſe account £2 2s. 0d. No more is now left in his hands. Voted, that each member of this Hunt do depoſit 29s. in the Secretary's hands for a fund to purchaſe Claret, and that Mr. Roger Wilbraham be requeſted to order it down, and that the Secretary do anſwer Mr. Roger Wilbraham's draft for that purpoſe.

"1779.—Oct. Rev. Mr. Lane and Mr. Whitworth are voted honorary members; it being the unanimous wiſh of the Society that the Rev. Mr. Lane as an original member, whenever he finds his health ſufficiently re-eſtabliſhed, may be conſidered a member of this Society. Agreed to allow Mr. Southon fifteenpence a bottle, and the bottles, for drinking our own claret.

"1780.—November. At this meeting a fox was found for the firſt time in the new gorſe cover, near the Old Pale.

"1782.—November. This Hunt, Mr. Beckford's Book on hunting being preſented by Mr. S. Arden in due form, the Secretary and two Aldermen attending, Mr. Egerton's Health was drunk in a bumper in a goblet.

"Offley Crewe and Sir P. Warburton were found

guilty of a most heinous offence in having crossed a hare's scut with a foxe's brush, and fined one gallon of Claret each, a very light fine for such an offence. Mr. R. Wilbraham prosecuted. Mr. Baugh was evidence, together with Mr. Peter Heron.

" 1783.—*November. This meeting a rule was made that the owner of the winning horse is not to give a dozen of Claret, as was customary.*

" *Mr. B. Grey, having moved that no cards or dice be allowed after the first toast after Supper, each member so offending against this rule must pay two dozen of Claret. The above rule was carried by a majority of four, the President being counted as two.*

" 1784.—*February. Ordered that the President's Chair be presented by the Tarporley Hunt to the Rev. Crewe Arden, the very worthy Rector of this Parish, as a testimony of their high respect and regard.*

" *November. Mr. T. Brooke, having been detected in making a wager in the dining Room, contrary to the rules of the Club, of £1 1s. 0d. to half-a-crown with Sir Peter Warburton, forfeited the wager.*

" *Mr. Grey having, at the request of the members present, undertaken to compile the different orders made by this Society, the books are to be delivered to him, with the thanks of the meeting, for the great trouble he is so good to take.*"

In 1773, *in the account of payments, is one of* £2 2s. 0d. *to* Mr. Yoxall, *for survey of intended alterations and plans. This, I presume, refers to the building of the new dining-room. In* 1775 *the sum of* £2 2s. *is given to two poor cottagers for losses by fire, and there is an entry of* 11s. 6d. *for advertising* Hunt.

In 1779 *the payment by the* Club *to* Crank *for* Mr. John Smith Barry's *picture is entered as follows :*

	£	s.	d.
" *Picture*	21	0	0
Frame	9	16	0
Case	1	19	0
Carriage of Picture . .	2	1	0 "

This picture is full length. At his master's feet sits Blue Cap, *the winner of the match at* Newmarket *in* 1762. *The portrait of the master is excellent, but the artist has been less successful in the hound.*

Crank, *who resided at* Warrington, *was at that time a well-known painter, and much patronised by the neighbouring gentry. I have been told that many years after his death, one of his pictures was sold as a portrait by* Gainsborough *for a large sum. As shown in the proceedings, Mr. Smith Barry had* "*politely consented to sit in* 1773." *Unless the order were delayed, the picture must have progressed but flowly, if only finished in* 1779; *poffibly the bill was not fent in till fome time after its completion.*

This compliment was paid to Mr. Smith Barry as *Mafter of Foxhounds, the firft pack known in Chefhire, and fupported entirely at his own ex-penfe.*

The following is the account of the above-named match, as given in Daniel's "*Rural Sports*," *vol. i. p.* 155: "*The fpeed of the Foxhound was well afcertained by the trial at Newmarket, between Mr. Meynell and Mr. Barry, and this account of the training and feeding the two Victorious Hounds is from the perfon who had the management of them. Will Crane was applied to, after the match was made (which was for* 500 *guineas), to train Mr. Barry's Hounds, of which* Blue Cap *was four, and* Wanton *three years old. Crane objected to their being hounds that had been entered fome feafons, and wifhed for young hounds, who would with more certainty be taught to run a Drag; how-ever, the hounds were fent to Rivenhall in Effex, and, as Crane fuggefted, at the firft trial, to induce them to run the drag, they took no notice; at length, by dragging a Fox along the ground, and then croff-ing the hounds upon the fcent, and taking care to let them kill him, they became very handy to a Drag, and had their exercife regularly three times a week upon Tiptree Heath; the ground chofen was Turf, and the diſtance over which the drag was taken was from eight to ten miles. The training commenced the firſt of Auguſt, and continued until the 28th of September (the thirtieth the match was run) ; their food was oatmeal and milk and ſheep's trotters. Upon the thirtieth of September the drag was drawn (on account of running up the wind, which happened to be briſk) from the Rubbing Houſe at Newmarket Town End, to the Rubbing Houſe at the ſtarting-poſt of the Beacon Courſe ; the four hounds were then laid on the ſcent ; Mr. Barry's* Blue Cap *came in firſt,* Wanton (*very cloſe to* Blue Cap) *ſecond ; Mr. Meynell's* Richmond *was beat by upwards of an hundred yards, and the Bitch never run in at all ; the ground was croſs'd in a few ſeconds more than eight minutes.[1] Three ſcore horſes ſtarted with the hounds. Cooper, Mr. Barry's Huntſman, was the firſt up, but the mare that carried him was rode quite blind at the concluſion. There were only twelve horſes up out of the Sixty ; and Will Crane, who was mounted upon a King's plate Horſe, called Rib, was in the twelfth. The odds before running were ſeven to four in favour of Mr. Meynell, whoſe hounds, it was ſaid, were fed*

---

[1] *Daniel does not give the year in which this match took place. The letterpreſs under a print in my poſſeſſion, engraved from a picture of the race, by Sartorius, ſtates that it was run in October, 1762, over the Beacon Courſe.*

during the time of training entirely with legs of mutton."

After the death of John Smith Barry, in 1784, *foxhounds were kept at Arley by Sir Peter War-burton, and, probably as owner of the pack, a similar request was made to him to sit for his picture, a full length by Sir William Beechey, for which the Hunt paid £250 in* 1811. *Sir William is said to have protested against the uniform, and to have declared he might as well be asked to paint a parrot.*

Since the date of the proceedings which close the two first books there have been but few changes in the rules of the Club. The earliest notice in the Racing Calendar of the Tarporley Races, held at Crabtree Green, is in 1776. *On the inclosure of Delamere Forest, in* 1812, *the present racecourse was rented from Lord Shrewsbury.*

In 1806 *it was agreed unanimously that the members .should subscribe the sum of £3 3s. each the next year for silver forks. It may appear strange to our ideas that a luxury, now so universal, should not have been introduced at Tarporley until the year* 1806; *but I am assured by a lady now living, that so late as* 1809, *in one of the most hospitable houses in the county, a silver fork was never seen on the dinner-table.*

The number of the members was eventually. in-creased to forty, and there is scarcely an old family

*name in the county which has not at some period
been enrolled on the lift.*

In the year 1862 *the centenary anniverfary of
the Club was celebrated; an additional fum was
given to the Farmers' Stakes, and the whole county
were invited by the members to a ball, held at the
Grofvenor Hotel, Chefter.*

*The "Chefhire Hounds," an eftablifhment quite
diftinct from the Tarporley Club, originated with
the pack kept by Sir Peter Warburton. It feems that
James Smith Barry, who fucceeded to his uncle's
property in* 1784, *and continued to keep hounds,
having in fome way offended the county gentlemen,
in the year* 1798 *Mr. Egerton of Tatton, Sir Peter
Warburton, Sir Richard Brooke, and, I believe,
Mr. Brooke of Mere, built the kennels at Sandiway, to which the hounds were removed from Arley.*

*Mr. Smith Barry ftill kept his pack, and lived
during the hunting feafon at Ruloe. I have heard
from an old refident in that neighbourhood a ftory
which, if true, fhows that he muft have hunted
under the difficulty of having no country beyond the
limits of his own property, and the fhifts to which
he was confequently compelled to refort. Old Richard
Bratt, his huntfman, was conftantly in the practice
of hiring a man to run a drag early in the morning
from the kennel at Ruloe ftraight away to fome
cover belonging to the Chefhire Hunt. The fcent*

carried the hounds into the gorfe, and fo gave the chance of finding a fox in a cover which their mafter had no right to draw.

I cannot afcertain in what year Sir Peter War-burton refigned the management of the Chefhire Hounds to George Heron; but the following anecdote in Daniel's "Rural Sports," vol. iii. p. 456, fhows that they were hunted by Sir Peter as late as 1807.

" To prove that the notes of hounds have an over-powering influence upon the horfe, this incident, which occurred Anno 1807, is related: As the Liverpool Mail Coach was changing horfes at the inn at Monk's Heath, the horfes which had per-formed the ftage from Congleton having been juft taken off and feparated, hearing Sir Peter War-burton's Foxhounds in full cry, immediately ftarted after, their harnefs on, and followed the chafe until the laft. One of them, a blood-mare, kept the track with the whipper-in, and gallantly followed him for about two hours over every leap he took, until Rey-nard run to earth in Mr. Hibbert's plantation. Thefe fpirited horfes were led back to the inn at Monk's Heath, and performed their ftage back to Congleton the fame evening."

George Heron held the management until 1818, but in confequence of a bad fall, by which he was difabled, Sir Harry Mainwaring, who eventually fucceeded him, had undertaken the field management in 1813.

Sir Harry, after a reign of nineteen years, gave them up in 1837. His firſt huntſman was Will Garſt, who left in Auguſt, 1820, when John Jones took his place, coming from Lord Scarborough, and continued until May, 1823. Will Head, who had been educated under Sir Bellingham Graham, and had been firſt whip to the Cheſhire for three ſeaſons, then obtained his promotion, and continued to hunt them until May, 1832. A letter from the late Sir Harry Mainwaring, containing theſe particulars, ends thus :—" In 1832 Joſeph Maiden came from Mr. Shaw, and remained with me until I gave up the hounds, Auguſt, 1837, continuing with other managers—a firſt-rate huntſman and a moſt excellent ſervant in every reſpeƈt." It is with great pleaſure that I record this teſtimony to the charaƈter of one who ſo well deſerv'd it. I cannot give the young foxhunter a better ſummary of the ſport (which had then, I think, reached its climax) than is contained in the following letter, addreſſed to the preſent Sir H. Mainwaring, which I have permiſſion to pub-liſh :—

" Withington Hall,
" January 10th, 1865.
" Dear Sir Harry,
" In the early days of the Nantwich Coun-try, from 1805 onwards, there was great ſport from Ravenſmoor to the Hills. Leech was conſtantly on

them, and we hardly ever failed in finding in the
Admiral's cover, and going direct as a line over
that fine country. I don't ever recollect to have seen
finer sport constantly than at that time and over
that country. The hounds then hunted the Woore
Country, and had a wonderful run from Buerton
Gorse, went thro' Oakley Park (Sir J. Chetwood's),
crossed the Drayton Road below the Loggerheads,
just skirted the Burnt Woods, left the Bishop's Woods
on the left, Hales on the left, right on thro' the
small woods at Knighton, and kill'd at Batchacre
Park (Mr. Whitworth's in Shropshire), 18 miles
as the crow flies, in an hour and forty-five minutes.
It was an extraordinary fine run, and to within
these few years that fox's pad was on the stable door
here. About the same time the hounds had a run of
about the same distance from Old Baddiley thro'
Cholmondeley, Dods-Edge, to the Shocklach meadows
and over the Dee, but Reynard got safe into Wales,
and it was too late at night to follow him any
further.

" So much for the Nantwich Country ! But in
Will Head's time we had as good a run as I ever
wish'd to see. We found at the Long Lane, in
Holford, hunted slowly thro' Winnington Wood, the
Leonards, Holbrook's nursery ground, up to the ice
house at Tabley; here he waited, having been bred
in the roof of it. From this point we had one of the

moſt continuous fine runs poſſible, croſſed the turnpike road cloſe to the lodge, to Tabley Walk, over Tabley High Fields, left Mere Moſs juſt to his right, thro' Gleave's Hole, over Winterbottom to Waterleſs Brook, where Brooke's Gorſe now ſtands, over the brook, which was rather a puzzler for the Field, but I ſaw where there was good getting out, and jumped in. When I got to the top of the bank every hound croſſed me at an open rail place. With this bother at the brook of courſe the hounds beat the Field, which did not come up till they were croſſing Budworth Heath. We then went behind Belmont, croſſed the Warrington Road, run down to the Horns at Whitley, where we kill'd, after a firſt-rate run.

" The ſplitting run over the Cheſter Vale, from Waverton Gorſe, was ſeen by few, when John Armitſtead's old black horſe, and "J.B. Glegg" had the credit of beating the Field. In Leiceſterſhire for pace and country I never ſaw a more brilliant affair. Rowland Warburton himſelf will recollect a capital ſpin we had from his own wood, croſſed the paved road a little above the Gore Bridge (all the Field went with the hounds ſave himſelf, Maiden, Self, and one or two others). Knowing where the cover was we put ſteam on, went down the road to the ford, and when we got to the top of the Gore Wood the hounds came out under our feet. From this point

to *Tatton Park* we were never caught. The fox then went acrofs to the *Birkin Lodge*, and up the middle of the *Park* to the garden at the houfe, where he was killed, after a mofl brilliant affair. *R.* *Warburton* will alfo recolleĉt a good run from the *Breeches*, when one of the twin brothers, *Peel*, loft his horfe direĉtly after leaving the cover; *Rowland's* advice was :—

> *" May you the next time that white horfe you beftraddle,*
> *See lefs of the Breeches and more of the Saddle."*

In the fame neighbourhood, in *Maiden's* time, we had a fplendid run from *Radnor Gorfe*, when *Mr.* *Knight* was knock'd off his horfe at the end of the firft field, and was ridden over by the crowd. The fox fet his head ftraight for *Woodhay*, left the farm-houfe on his left, then up to *Chertfey's Wood*, croffed the wide green lane at the top, at which point the pace had thinned the Field very much. *Sir Richard Brooke*, on a big grey, fell, leaping into the road, and never got beyond. *Maiden* here ftopp'd the Corporal, and the running was left to *Clive of Stych*, *Coke Gooch*, and myfelf; but on going up the field, leaving *Alderfey's* rough on the left, the Colonel's grey put his foot in a grip, and went heels over head. The field then was quite beat off. We went on to *Bunbury*, then to the right, by *Wardle Hall*, and kill'd after an unufually fine run at *Rees Heath*. *Wilbraham Tollemache* ftopp'd the Rebel in the firft ten minutes.

Don't think this a very boasting detail of sport. The only thing I can do now is to go a little over the mahogany; but a long life of uninterrupted good health enabled me to be constantly out, and to carry my recollections of good runs as far back as most. But I must stop, for every good run were I to record, Sir, I ne'er should have done.

"*Yours truly,*
"*J. B. GLEGG.*"

The race over Tatton Park from Mobberly Cover, 4 miles in 8 minutes, was an extraordinary performance.

Sir Harry Mainwaring supplies me with some further particulars of about the same period :—

Jan. 12, 65.

"*In the palmy days of hunting in Cheshire it must be recollected that Glegg first refers to the time when George Heron kept the Hounds, when Will Garfit hunted them, and Will Griffiths whipp'd in, when Doddington, Dorfold, Bolesworth Castle and Bryn-y-Pys, were the chief hunting houses, when Crewe, Broughton, Tarleton, and (rather later on) Tomkinson, Brooke and Glegg were the heroes, when the Cheshire hunted the Woore Country and the Wyches, when they used to run as described by Glegg from Woore to the Bishop's Woods, and from*

d

Hampton Heath to the Duke's Woods, near Ellef-mere. Later on, when my Father took the Country, and the Wyches were given up, gorfes were made in the Nantwich Country, and in the Chefter Vale. The Middlewich Country, then as it is now, the beft in Chefhire, was hunted the fecond week in every month, and the Withington Country the laft week. The Withington Kennels were given up, and kennels built at Peover.

" Glegg has omitted the two beft runs I ever faw. We met at Hurleftone, and had drawn all the covers in the country blank, when (it was late in March, and Will Head, Huntfman) we found at 3 p.m., in a fmall patch of gorfe under Calveley Park wall, a very fmall Fox. The hounds got away clofe to him, and all went together into the barn at the farmhoufe ; ' the fox is kill'd,' we all faid, but he got away under the door. Head caft the hounds round the barn, away we went ! very beft pace ! over Wettenhall Green, up to the wood, left it and Darnhall on the left, and made a fudden turn to the right, over the very beft of the Minfhull Country, to the river at Eardfwick Hall, a mile above Minfhull Village. We croffed at the wooden bridge, and run very faft almoft to Bradfield Green, bore to the left, and we ran into our Fox, a fmall vixen without cubs, at Warmincham Rectory, one hour almoft without a check. James Tomkinfon rode ' The Pea,' and he mounted me on ' Whizgig.'

" *Maiden Huntfman, met at Afhley Hall, a cold day in March, high N. E. wind; fnow fell in the morning. Put the hounds into Cooper's Plantation, a fmall place, and immediately chopp'd a fine dog-fox. Another was halloo'd away at fame time, and away we went at a capital pace almoft up to Caftle Mill, turn'd to right, and then over a fine wild country, the beft of Mobberley, towards Wilmflow, over Lindon Common, Warford, Little Warford, and up to where Chelford Station now is, left Aftle on right, and away ftraight to Alderley Park, where I faw the hounds run into him under the Library Window dead beat; about an hour, a very good run, and many horfes beat.*

" *You will recollect a run in Ford's time, March 1, 1842, from the ' Cobbler ' up to the road at Whitley Reed, turn'd over Crowley Mofs, ftraight to Arley, over the bridge at Arley Green to the Gore, on to Tabley through the old Foxcover at Lower Peover where Maiden came up and they killed him at Gooftrey; only about eight men with the Hounds, the Field having been all thrown out at Whitley Reed.*"

Thefe indeed are runs to be remembered; without wifhing to fet myfelf up as a praifer of paft times I afk, do we ever hear of fuch now-a-day? I afk in forrow, not reproachfully; hounds, horfes, and huntf-men are probably as good, if not better than they formerly were, but every succeeding year seems to add some new impediment to Fox-hunting. High farming is rapidly converting our fields into gardens. " Look before you leap," is a precaution more requisite than ever since the introduction of wire fencing.

The increase of population and of dwellings prevents a fox, headed at every corner, from making straight to his point, and last but not least in the list of grievances is the scarcity of wild foxes.

A burst, such as that mentioned by Mr. Glegg, from Waverton Gorse may still excite us for ten or twenty minutes, but where do we read of such runs as that from Buerton, " eighteen miles as the crow flies in an hour and forty-five minutes ? "

It was in Sir Harry Mainwaring's time, on the 7th of April, 1829, that the meet of the three packs took place at Shavington. The Cheshire, the Shropshire and Mr. Wicksted's Kennel sent each six couple of hounds. The Cheshire being the oldest pack and the place of meeting being in the Cheshire country Will Head was appointed huntsman for the day, Will Staples the Shropshire huntsman, and " old Wells," who had command of Mr. Wicksted's kennel, were both in attendance. In the first run the fox was lost near Cloverly after a fast thirty minutes. Mytton took the lead and charged a post and rail, exclaiming " Now for the honour of Shropshire ! " He got a terrible fall, and was much hurt by another man jumping on him, there being about a dozen down together. Mytton remounted, bleeding and bare-headed, but was too much hurt to take another lead.

A second fox was found at Combermere, which was run for about twenty minutes, but, proving a vixen, the hounds were stopped.

Though Will Head and Staples claimed each the palm for their respective kennels, it would be difficult to say which Pack proved its superiority in that day's hunting.

On Sir Harry Mainwaring's resignation in 1837, the establishment was handed over to Mr. Shakerley of Whatcroft. Amongst the many good runs shown during the short time he conducted the Pack was that from Calveley, alluded to under the title of " Cheshire Chivalry." Mounted on his bay horse " Tatton," Mr. Shakerley figures as manager in the foreground of Calvert's Picture of the Cheshire Hunt. In 1839, Mr. Smith Barry of Marbury and Mr. Dixon of Astle undertook the control of the Kennel. Mr. Ford, of Abbey Field, who succeeded them, held the management for the season only of 1841, and resigned it into the hands of Mr. White.

" Leicestershire White," as he is called in Mr. Wicksted's Song, was known far and wide for many years as one of the best horsemen in England, whether in the racing or in the hunting saddle. After re-

tiring from the management, he ſtill occupied the Hunting Box, adjoining the Kennel, at Daleford. Continuing to hunt with the Cheſhire, and riding to the laſt as well as ever, he reſided there till his death in 1866.

In May, 1862, a portrait and memoir of him was publiſhed in " Baily's Magazine." Further particulars of his career were afterwards recorded in ſeveral ſporting periodicals, and an intereſting article appeared in the " Saturday Review," February, 1866, where, in a quotation, he is ſpoken of as having " left an undying reputation as a Gentleman Jockey and Fox-hunter."

His maſterſhip ceaſed in 1855, when the Pack was handed over to Captain Mainwaring. Owing to circumſtances to which it is needleſs here to allude, at the beginning of the Seaſon of 1856 many of the landowners warned the Hounds off their eſtates, and, in compliance with their wiſhes, the hunting men were compelled to ſubmit to the loſs of their ſport rather than cauſe a diſſenſſion in the county.

In 1858, the county was relieved from this difficulty by the acceſſion of Lord Groſvenor. The Eſtabliſhment in every department was kept up by him moſt efficiently, and our only regret was that his many other duties compelled him ſo often to be abſent from the field.

On the reſignation of Lord Groſvenor, in 1866,

Mr. Corbet, of Adderley, undertook the management of the hounds, stipulating that he should be allowed to hunt five instead of four days a-week.

Peter Collison, a very quick and active huntsman, retained his place with Mr. Corbet until 1869, when he was succeeded by John Jones, who had whipped in to him for several seasons.

I trust that, in describing the difficulties which now attend it, I have not drawn too gloomy a picture of the future of Fox-hunting. My best wishes are for its lasting prosperity, and whatever be the obstacles against which it may have to struggle, my earnest hope is that the youth of many generations to come may continue to find as much enjoyment as their forefathers have done in the noble sport.

HUNTING SONGS.

The Woore Country.

I.

NOW fummer's dull feafon is over,
 Once more we behold the glad
  pack;
And Wickfted appears at the cover,
 Once more on old Mercury's back;
And Wells in the faddle is feated,
 Though with fcarce a whole bone in his fkin;
His cheer by the echo repeated,
 'Loo in! little dearies! 'loo in!

II.

How eagerly forward they rufh,
 In a moment how widely they fpread;
Have at him there, Hotfpur! hufh! hufh!
 'Tis a find or I'll forfeit my head;

B

Faſt flies the Fox away—faſter
 The hounds from the cover are freed;
The horn to the mouth of the maſter,
 The ſpur to the flank of his ſteed.

III.

Through ages recorded in metre
 May the fame of each rider ſurvive;
From Tunſtall comes Broughton, call'd Peter,
 From Styche comes the brotherhood Clive.
There's Hammond from Wiſtaſton bringing
 All the news of the neighbouring ſhire;
Fitzherbert renown'd for his ſinging,
 And Dorfold's invincible Squire;

IV.

Few Sportſmen ſo gallant, if any,
 Did Woore ever ſend to the chaſe;
Each dingle for him has a cranny,
 Each river a fordable place;
He knows the beſt line from each cover,
 He knows where to ſtand for a ſtart,
And long may he live to ride over
 The country he loves in his heart.

V.

There's Henry, the purple-clad Vicar,
 So earneſtly plying the ſteel;
Conductor conducting him quicker,
 Each prick from the ſpur at his heel.

Were my life to depend on the wager,
   I know not which brother I'd back;
The Vicar, the Squire, or the Major,
   The Purple, the Pink, or the Black.

VI.

On a thorough-bred horſe there's a bruiſer,
   Intent upon taking a lead;
The name of the man is John Crewe, ſir,
   And Ajax the name of the ſteed;
There's Aqualate's Baronet, Boughey,
   Whoſe eye ſtill on Wickſted is caſt;
Should the Fox run till midnight, I know he
   Will ſtick by his friend to the laſt.

VII.

The Ford they call Charlie,—how cheery
   To ride by his ſide in a run;
Whether midnight or morn, never weary
   Of revel, and frolic, and fun.
When they lay this good fellow the tomb in,
   He ſhall not be mock'd with a buſt,
But the favourite evergreen blooming
   Shall ſpring and o'erſhadow his duſt.

VIII.

With Choriſter, Concord, and Chorus,
   Now Chantreſs commences her ſong,
Now Bellman goes jingling before us,
   And Sinbad is ſailing along;

Old Wells clofely after them cramming,
  His foul quite abforb'd in the fun,
Continues unconfcioufly damning
  Their dear little hearts as they run.

IX.

Scent on the fallow now failing,
  While onward impatiently prefs
The horfemen—hear Charlie bewailing
  In accents of bitter diftrefs—
" Why, why will you fpoil me the day now ;
  Have they run but to lofe him at laft ?
Pray now, friends ! gentlemen ! pray now,
  Hold hard, let them make their own caft."

X.

One moment for breathing we tarry,
  One caft and they hit it anew ;
See ! fee ! what a head they now carry,
  And fee now they run him in view.
More eager for blood at each ftroke,
  See Vengeance and Vulpicide rufh ;
Poor Renard, he thinks it no joke,
  Hearing Joker fo clofe at his brufh.

XI.

See ! Soldier prepar'd for the brunt,
  Hark !   Champion's challenge I hear ;
While Victory leads them in front,
  And Havock purfues in the rear ;

Whoop-hoop! they have ended the fkurry,
   And Charlie half mad with the run,
Firft dances and fhouts, " Worry ! worry !"
   Then tells what each darling has done.

XII.

A fig for your Leicefterfhire fwells !
   While Wickfted fuch fport can enfure ;
Long life to that varmint old Wells !
   Succefs to the country of Woore !
Let Statefmen on politics parley,
   Let Heroes go fight for renown,
While I've health to go hunting with Charley,
   I envy no Monarch his crown.
                    1830.

Quæfitum Meritis.

I.

A CLUB of good fellows we meet once a year,
   When the leaves of the foreft are yellow
       and fear ;
By the motto that fhines on each glafs, it is
       fhown,
We pledge in our cups the deferving alone ;
Our glafs a quæfitum, ourfelves Chefhire men,
May we fill it and drink it again and again.

II.

We hold in abhorrence all vulpicide knaves,
With their gins, and their traps, and their velveteen
    flaves ;
They may feed their fat pheafants, their foxes de-
    ftroy,
And mar the prime fport they themfelves can't
    enjoy ;
But fuch fportfmen as thefe we good fellows con-
    demn,
And I vow we'll ne'er drink a quæfitum to them.

III.

That man of his wine is unworthy indeed,
Who grudges to mount a poor fellow in need ;
Who keeps for nought elfe, fave to purge 'em
    with balls,
Like a dog in a manger, his nags in their ftalls ;
Such niggards as thefe we good fellows condemn,
And I vow we'll ne'er drink a quæfitum to them.

IV.

Some riders there are, who, too jealous of place,
Will fling back a gate in their next neighbour's
    face ;
Some never pull up when a friend gets a fall,
Some ride over friends, hounds, and horfes, and
    all ;

Such riders as thefe we good fellows condemn,
And I vow we'll ne'er drink a quæfitum to them.

V.

For coffee-houfe goffip fome hunters come out,
Of all matters prating, fave that they're about;
From fcandal and cards they to politics roam,
They ride forty miles, head the Fox, and go
    home!
Such fportfmen as thefe we good fellows
    condemn,
And I vow we'll ne'er drink a quæfitum to them.

VI.

Since one Fox on foot more diverfion will bring
Than twice twenty thoufand cock pheafants on
    wing,
The man we all honour, whate'er be his rank,
Whofe heart heaves a figh when his gorfe is
    drawn blank.
Quæfitum! Quæfitum! fill up to the brim,
We'll drink, if we die for't, a bumper to him.

VII.

O! give me that man to whom nought comes
    amifs,
One horfe or another, that country or this;

Through falls and bad ftarts who undauntedly
    ftill
Rides up to this motto: " Be with 'em I will."
Quæfitum ! Quæfitum ! fill up to the brim,
We'll drink, if we die for't, a bumper to him.

VIII.

O ! give me that man who can ride through a
    run,
Nor engrofs to himfelf all the glory when done;
Who calls not each horfe that o'ertakes him a
    " fcrew,"
Who loves a run beft when a friend fees it too !
Quæfitum ! Quæfitum ! fill up to the brim,
We'll drink, if we die for't, a bumper to him.

IX.

O ! give me that man who himfelf goes the pace,
And whofe table is free to all friends of the
    chafe ;
Should a fpirit fo choice in this wide world be
    feen,
He rides, you may fwear, in a collar of green ;
Quæfitum ! Quæfitum ! fill up to the brim,
We'll drink, if we die for't, a bumper to him.

                             1832.

Old Oulton Lowe.

I.

BAD luck to the Country! the clock had ftruck
two,
We had found ne'er a Fox in the gorfes we drew;
When each heart felt a thrill at the found,
" Tally-Ho ! "
Once more a view hollo from old Oulton Lowe!

II.

Away like a whirlwind toward Calveley Hall,
For the firft thirty minutes Pug laugh'd at us all;
Our nags cur'd of kicking, ourfelves of conceit,
Ere the laugh was with us, we were moft of us
beat.

III.

The Willington mare, when fhe ftarted fo faft,
Ah! we little thought then that the race was her
laft ;
Accurft be the ftake that was ftain'd with her
blood ;
But why cry for fpilt milk ?—may the next be as
good !

IV.

'Twas a fight for us all, worth a million, I fwear,
To fee the Black Squire how he rode the black
mare ;

The meed that he merits, the Mufe fhall beftow,
Firft, foremoft, and fleeteft from old Oulton
    Lowe!

V.

How Delamere went, it were ufelefs to tell,
To fay he was out, is to fay he went well;
A rider fo fkilful ne'er buckled on fpur
To rule a rafh horfe, or to make a fcrew ftir.

VI.

The odds are in fighting that Britain beats France;
In the chafe, as in war, we muft all take our
    chance.
Little Ireland kept up, like his namefake the
    nation,
By dint of " coercion " and great " agitation."

VII.

Now Victor and Bedford were feen in the van,
Cheer'd on by the Maiden who rides like a man,
He fcreech'd with delight as he wip'd his hot
    brow,
" Their briftles are up! Sir! they're hard at him
    now."

VIII.

In the pride of his heart, then the Manager cried,
" Come along, little Rowley boy, why don't you
    ride ? "

How he chuckled to fee the long tail in diftrefs,
As he gave her the go-by on bonny brown Befs.

IX.

The Baron from Hanover hollow'd "whoo-hoop,"
While he thought on the Lion that eat him half
    up;
Well pleas'd to have balk'd the wild beaft of his
    dinner,
He was up in his ftirrups, and rode like a winner.

X.

Oh! where 'mid the many found wanting in fpeed,
Oh! where and oh! where was the Wiftafton
    fteed?
Dead beat! ftill his rider fo lick'd him and prick'd
    him,
He thought (well he might) 'twas the Devil that
    kick'd him.

XI.

The Ceftrian cheftnut fhow'd fymptoms of blood,
For it flow'd from his nofe ere he came to the
    wood.
Where now is Dollgofh? Where the racer from
    Da'enham?
Such faft ones as thefe! what mifhap has o'er-
    ta'en 'em?

XII.

Two gentlemen met, both unhors'd, in a lane,
(Fox-hunting on foot is but labour in vain,)
"Have you feen a brown horfe?" "No, indeed,
    Sir; but pray,
In the courfe of your ramble have *you* feen a
    grey?"

XIII.

As a London coal-heaver might pick up a peer,
Whom he found in the ftreet, with his head
    rather queer,
So Dobbin was loos'd from his work at the plough,
To affift a proud hunter, ftuck faft in a flough.

XIV.

I advocate "movement" when fhown in a horfe,
But I love in my heart a "confervative" gorfe;
Long life to Sir Philip! we'll drink ere we go,
Old times! and old Chefhire! and old Oulton
    Lowe!

             1833.

Tarporley Hunt, 1833.

I.

WHEN without verdure the woods in No-
    vember are,
  Then to our collars their green is transferr'd;
Racing and chafing the fports of each member are,
  Come then to Tarporley booted and fpurr'd;

Holding together, Sir,
Scorning the weather, Sir,
Like the good leather, Sir,
    Which we put on:
Quæfitum meritis!
Good fun how rare it is!
I know not where it is,
    Save at the Swan.

II.

Lo! there's a Maiden whofe fweet difpofition is
    Bent, like Diana's of old, on the chafe;
Joy to that fportfman whofe horfe, in condition, is
    Able and willing to go the beft pace;
        Racers are fweating now,
        Owners are fretting now,
        Stable boys betting now,
           France! ten to one:
    Quæfitum meritis, &c.

III.

Lo! where the foreft turf covers gentility,
    Foremoft with glory and hindmoft with mud;
Now let the Prefident prove his ability,
    Umpire of fpeed, whether cocktail or blood;
        Go-by and Adelaide,
        Though they were faddled,
        Led forth and ftraddled,
           Judge there was none!
    Quæfitum meritis, &c.

IV.

How with due praife fhall I fing the Palatinate,
  Ably with Prefidents filling our chair ;
The Greys and the Leghs, and the Brookes that
    have fat in it,
  Toafting our bumpers and drinking their fhare?
      Each Squire and each Lord, Sir,
      That meets at our board, Sir,
      Were I to record, Sir,
        I ne'er fhould have done :
      Quæfitum meritis, &c.

V.

" Sume fuperbiam quæfitam meritis,"
  Shades of Sir Peter and Barry look down,
Long may we good fellows, now a day rarities,
  Live to make merry in Tarporley town.
      Fox prefervation,
      Throughout the whole nation,
      Affords recreation,
        Then drink it, each man :
      Quæfitum meritis !
      Good fun how rare it is !
      I know not where it is,
        Save at the Swan.

The Little Red Rover.

I.

THE dewdrop is clinging
  To whin-bufh and brake,
The fkylark is finging
  "Merrie hunters, awake;"
Home to the cover,
  Deferted by night,
The little Red Rover
  Is bending his flight.

II.

Refounds the glad hollo;
  The pack fcents the prey;
Man and horfe follow
  Away! Hark, away!
Away! never fearing,
  Ne'er flacken your pace:
What mufic fo cheering
  As that of the chafe?

III.

The Rover ftill fpeeding,
  Still diftant from home,
Spurr'd flanks are bleeding,
  And cover'd with foam;

Fleet limbs extended,
   Roan, cheftnut, or grey,
The burft, ere 'tis ended,
   Shall try them to-day!

IV.

Well known is yon cover,
   And crag hanging o'er,
The little Red Rover
   Shall reach it no more!
The foremoft hounds near him,
   His ftrength 'gins to droop :
In pieces they tear him,
   Who-whoop ! Who-who-whoop!

The Fox and the Brambles.

A FABLE.

BEFORE the pack for many a mile
   A Fox had fped in gallant ftyle;
But gafping with fatigue at laft,
The clamorous hounds approach'd him faft ;
Though painful now the toilfome race,
With draggled brufh and ftealthy pace
Still onward for his life he flies—
He nears the wood—before him lies
A tangled mafs of thorn and bramble ;
In vain beneath he tries to fcramble,

So fpringing, heedlefs of his fkin,
With defperate bound he leaps within.
The prickly thicket o'er him clofes ;
To him it feem'd a bed of rofes,
As there he lay and heard around
The baying of the baffled hound.
Within that bufh, his fears allay'd,
He many a fage reflection made ;
" 'Tis true, whene'er I ftir," he cried,
" The brambles wound my bleeding fide,
" But he who feeks may feek in vain
" For perfect blifs ; then why complain ?
" Since, mingled in one current, flow
" Both good and evil, joy and woe ;
" O ! let me ftill with patience bear
" The evil, for the good that's there.
" Howe'er unpleafant this retreat,
" Yet every bitter has its fweet ;
" The brambles pierce my fkin, no doubt,
" The hounds had torn my entrails out."

Good farmers ! read, nor take amifs,
The moral which I draw from this ;
Grieve not o'er gap or broken gate ;
The damage fmall, the profit great ;
The love of fport to home brings down
Your Landlord from the fmoky town,
To dwell and fpend his rents among

The tenantry, from whom they fprung.
Though vainly when he leads the chafe,
His willing fteed urged on apace,
When fcent is good and hounds are fleet,
Though vainly then you fhout, " Ware wheat!"
That fteed, perchance, by you was bred,
And yours the corn on which he's fed ;
Ah ! then reftrain your rifing ire,
Nor rafhly damn the Hunting Squire.

The Earth Stopper.

I.

TERROR of henroofts ! now from hollow
fand-earth,
Safely at nightfall, round the quiet farmftead,
Reynard on tiptoe, meditating plunder,
        Warily prowleth.

II.

Roufe thee ! Earth ftopper ! roufe thee from thy
        flumber !
Get thee thy worfted hofe and winter coat on,
While the good houfewife, crawling from her
        blanket,
        Lights thee thy lantern.

III.

Clad for thy midnight filent occupation,
Mount thy old doghorfe, fpade upon thy fhoulder,
Wiry hair'd Vixen, wherefoe'er thou wendeft,
    Ready to follow.

IV.

Though the chill rain drops, driven by the north
    wind,
Pelt thy old jacket, foaking through and through
    thee,
Though thy worn hackney, blind and broken
    winded,
        Hobble on three legs;

V.

Finifh thy night-work well, or woe betide thee,
If on the morrow irritated Huntfman,
Back'd by a hundred followers in fcarlet,
        Find the earths open!

The Old Brown Foreſt.

I.

BROWN Foreſt of Mara! whofe bounds
    were of yore
From Kellfborrow's Caſtle outſtretch'd to the
    fhore,

Our fields and our hamlets afforefted then,
That thy beafts might have covert—unhous'd
   were our men.

II.

Our King the firft William, Hugh Lupus our
   Earl,
Then poaching, I ween, was no fport for a churl;
A noofe for his neck who a fnare fhould contrive,
Who fkinn'd a dead buck was himfelf flay'd alive !

III.

Our Normandy nobles right dearly, I trow,
They loved in the foreft to bend the yew bow;
They wound their " recheat " and their " mort "
   on the horn,
And they laugh'd the rude chafe of the Saxon to
   fcorn.

IV.

In right of his bugle and greyhounds, to feize
Waif, pannage, agiftment and windfallen trees,
His knaves through our foreft Ralph Kingfley
   difpers'd,
Bow-bearer in chief to Earl Randle the firft.

V.

This horn the Grand Forefter wore at his fide
Whene'er his liege lord chofe a hunting to ride;
By Sir Ralph and his heirs for a century blown,
It pafs'd from their lips to the mouth of a Done.

VI.

O! then the proud falcon, unloos'd from the
    glove,
Like her mafter below, play'd the tyrant above;
While faintly, more faintly, were heard in the fky,
The filver-ton'd bells as fhe darted on high.

VII.

Then rous'd from fweet flumber, the ladie high
    born,
Her palfrey would mount at the found of the horn;
Her palfrey uptofs'd his rich trappings in air,
And neigh'd with delight fuch a burden to bear.

VIII.

Vers'd in all woodcraft and proud of her fkill,
Her charms in the foreft feem'd lovelier ftill;
The Abbot rode forth from the abbey fo fair,
Nor lov'd the fport lefs when a bright eye was
    there.

IX.

Thou Palatine prophet! whofe fame I revere
(Woe be to that bard who fpeaks ill of a feer),
Forewarn'd of thy fate, as our legends report,
Thou wert born in a foreft and " clemm'd " in
    a court.

X.

Now goading thine oxen, now urging amain
Fierce monarchs to battle on Bofworth's red plain;

" A foot with two heels, and a hand with three
    thumbs ! "
Good luck to the land when this prodigy comes!

XI.

" Steeds fhall by hundreds feek mafters in vain,
Till under their bellies the girths rot in twain ; "
'Twill need little fkill to interpret this dream,
When o'er the brown foreft we travel by fteam !

XII.

Here hunted the Scot whom, too wife to fhow
    fight,
No war, fave the war of the woods, could excite ;
His learning, they fay, did his valour furpafs,
Though a hero when arm'd with a couteau de
    chaffe.

XIII.

Ah ! then came the days when to England's
    difgrace,
A King was her quarry, and warfare her chafe ;
Old Noll for their huntfman ! a puritan pack !
With pfalms on their tongues—but with blood
    in their track.

XIV.

Then Charlie our King was reftor'd to his own,
And again the blythe horn in the foreft was blown ;
Steeds from the defert then crofs'd the blue wave
To contend on our turf for the prizes he gave.

XV.

Ere Bluecap and Wanton taught fox-hounds to
    fkurry,
With mufic in plenty—O! where was the hurry?
When each nag wore a crupper, each Squire a
    pigtail;
When our toaft "The Brown Foreft," was drunk
    in brown ale.

XVI.

The faft ones came next, with a wild fox in view,
"Ware hole!" was a caution then heeded by few;
Oppos'd by no cops, by no fences confin'd,
O'er whinbufh and heather they fwept like the
    wind.

XVII.

Behold! in the foil of our foreft once more,
The fapling takes root as in ages of yore;
The oak of old England with branches outfpread,
The pine-tree above them uprearing its head.

XVIII.

Where, 'twixt the whalebones, the widow fat
    down,
Who forfook the Black foreft to dwell in the
    Brown,
There, where the flock on fweet herbage once fed,
The blackcock takes wing, and the fox-cub is bred.

XIX.

This timber the ftorms of the ocean fhall weather,
And fail o'er the waves as we fail'd o'er the
    heather;
Each plant of the foreft, when launch'd from the
    ftocks,
May it run down a foeman as we do a Fox.

The Dead Hunter.

I.

HIS fire from the defert, his dam from the
    north,
The pride of my ftable ftept gallantly forth,
One flip in his ftride as the fcurry he led,
And my fteed, ere his rivals o'ertook him, lay
    dead.

II.

Poor fteed! fhall thy limbs on the hunting field
    lie,
That his beak in thy carcafe the raven may dye?
Is it thine the fad doom of thy race to fulfil,
Thy flefh to the cauldron, thy bones to the mill?

III.

Ah! no.—I beheld thee a foal yet unfhod,
Now race round the paddock, now roll on the fod;

Where firſt thy young hoof the green herbage
  imprefs'd,
There, the ſhoes on thy feet, will I lay thee to
  reſt !

The Spectre Stag.

A LEGEND OF THE RHINE.

I.

A BARON lived in Germany,
  Of old and noble race,
Whofe mind was wholly bent upon
  The pleafures of the chafe.

II.

Thro' fummer's fultry dog-days,
  Thro' winter's froſt fevere,
This Baron's hunting feafon
  Was twelve months in the year.

III.

From dawn till dark he hunted,
  And the truth I grieve to fpeak,
The number of his hunting days
  Was feven in the week.

IV.

No lands within his feignorie
  Was ferf allowed to till ;

No corn-field in the valley,
　No vineyard on the hill.

V.

What marvel hungry poachers,
　When the Baron was a-bed,
Were bent on ſtealing veniſon,
　For very lack of bread?

VI.

But woe that wretch betided,
　Who in the queſt was found;
On the ſtag he would have ſlaughter'd
　Was his naked body bound.

VII.

Borne, like Mazeppa, headlong,
　From the panting quarry's back
He ſaw the thirſty blood-hounds
　Let looſe upon his track.

VIII.

The pack, their prey o'ertaken,
　On the mangled victims feaſt;
And, mix'd in one red ſlaughter,
　Flows the blood of man and beaſt.

IX.

The Baron thus his paſtime
　Purſued until he died;
My tale ſhall tell how this befell
　On the eve of Eaſtertide.

X.

The moon rofe o'er the foreft,
    And the diftant village chime
Call'd finners to confeffion,
    And befpoke a hallow'd time.

XI.

When fuddenly a ftrange halloo
    Was heard around to ring,
The Hunter feiz'd his bow and plac'd
    An arrow on the ftring.

XII.

The cry, the cheer, the tumult
    Of the chafe—and then, difplay'd
By the pale light of the moonbeam,
    Far adown the foreft-glade,

XIII.

Was feen, with brow full antler'd,
    A Monfter Stag—his back
Beftridden by a Huntfman,
    Apparell'd all in black.

XIV.

Their eyes unto their mafter
    The crouching pack uprais'd,
Their mafter on his trembling fteed
    At the fight was fore amaz'd.

XV.

"Ye curs," he cried, "why ftir ye not?
A curfe upon the breed!
And you, ye loitering varlets,
    Where are ye in fuch need?"

XVI.

To fummon then his followers,
    He grafp'd his hunting horn,
Through the foreft's deep receffes
    The echoing blaft was borne.

XVII.

But borne in vain—his retinue
    No note in anfwer gave;
And the filence that fucceeded
    Was the filence of the grave.

XVIII.

His eye in terror glancing
    From glade to diftant crag,
Nought faw he fave the fpectre
    Goading on that grifly ftag.

XIX.

The nearer it approach'd him,
    The larger ftill it grew;
Again he feiz'd his hunting horn,
    And his gafping breath he drew.

XX.

Eye, cheek, and throat diftended,
Each fibre ftrain'd to blow,
His life-breath paft in that bugle blaft,
And he fell from the faddle bow.

XXI.

Where the Baron's chafe was ended,
There they laid his bones to rot ;
And his heirs, in after ages,
Built a Chapel on the fpot.

XXII.

And ftill, they fay, that bugle blaft,
When Eafter-tide comes round,
Difturbs the midnight foreft
With a ftrange unearthly found.

On the New Kennel, erected on

Delamere Foreft.

MAY, 1834.

I.

G REAT names in the Abbey are graven in
ftone,
Our kennel records them in good flefh and bone;
A *Bedford*, a *Glofter*, to life we reftore,
And *Nelfon* with *Victory* couple once more,
    Derry down, down, down, derry down.

II.

Were the laws of the kennel the laws of the land,
The ſhillalah ſhould drop from the Iriſhman's
    hand ;
And journeymen tailors, on "ſtriking" intent,
Should ſtick to their ſtitching like hounds to a
    ſcent.

III.

O ! grant, ye reformers, who rule o'er us all,
That our kennels may ſtand though our colleges
    fall ;
Our pack from long trial we know to be good,
Grey-hounds admitted might ruin the blood.

IV.

Fond parents may dote on their pride of thirteen,
Switch'd into Latin and breech'd in nankeen ;
A puppy juſt enter'd a language can ſpeak
More ſweetly ſonorous than Homer's own
    Greek.

V.

O ! clothe me in ſcarlet ! a ſpur on each heel !
And guardſmen may caſe their whole bodies in
    ſteel !
Lancers in battle with lancers may tilt,
Mine be the warfare unſullied with guilt !

VI.

New built, may this kennel continue to rear
A pack ſtill as prime as the old ones bred here ;
May the depth of their cry be no check to their
pace,
But the ring of their muſic ſtill gladden the chaſe.
Derry down, down, down, derry down.
1834.

The Ladie Cunigunda of Kynaſt.

TRANSLATED FROM THE GERMAN.

(F. RUCKERT.)

I.

" IN my bower," ſaid Cunigunda,
    "No longer will I bide,
I will ride forth to the hunting,
    Right merrie 'tis to ride."

II.

Said ſhe, " None but a valiant Knight
    Shall win me for a bride ;
Undaunted muſt he venture
    Round my caſtle wall to ride."

III.

Then rode a noble Knight along
    The Kynaſt Caſtle wall ;

Her hand that Ladie rais'd not
  At the noble Knight's downfall.

IV.

Upon that wall another Knight
  Rode gallantly and well;
That Ladie's heart mifgave her not
  When horfe and rider fell.

V.

Another Knight, and once again
  Another dar'd to try,
And both, down rolling headlong,
  She beheld with tearlefs eye.

VI.

Thus years and years pafs'd on, until
  No Knight again drew nigh;
None to ride again would venture,
  For to venture was to die.

VII.

Cunigunda from the battlement
  Look'd out both far and wide:
" I fit within my bower alone,
  Will none attempt the ride?

VIII.

" O! is there none would win me now,
  And wear me for a bride?
Has chivalry turn'd recreant?
  Has knighthood loft its pride?"

IX.

Out fpake Thuringia's Landgrave
(Count Adelbert he hight,)
"This Ladie fair is worthy well
The venture of a Knight."

X.

The Landgrave train'd his war-horfe
On the mountain fteep to go,
That the Ladie might not glory
In another overthrow.

XI.

"'Tis I, O noble Ladie,
Who will on the venture fpeed;"
Sadly, earneftly, fhe eyed him,
As he fprang upon his fteed.

XII.

She faw him mount and onward fpur,
She trembled and fhe figh'd:
"O woe is me that for my fake
He tries this fearful ride!"

XIII.

He rode along the caftle wall,
She turn'd her from the fight:
"Woe is me, he rideth ftraightway
To his grave, that noble Knight!"

D

XIV.

He rode along the caſtle wall,
  On dizzy rampart there;
She dar'd not move a finger
  Of her hand, that Ladie fair!

XV.

He rode along the caſtle wall,
  O'er battlement and mound;
She dar'd not breathe a whiſper,
  Leſt he totter at the ſound.

XVI.

He rode around the caſtle wall,
  And down again rode he:
" Now God be prais'd that he hath ſpar'd
  Thy precious life to thee!

XVII.

" May God be prais'd thou didſt not ride
  A death-ride to thy grave!
Now quit thy ſteed and claim thy bride,
  Thou worthy Knight and brave!"

XVIII.

Then ſpake the Landgrave, bending down
  Unto the ſaddle bow:
" That Knight can dare, O Ladie fair,
  This morning's ride doth ſhow.

XIX.

"Wait thou until another come
To do this feat for thee;
A wife I have and children,
And my bride thou canſt not be."

XX.

He ſpurr'd his ſteed and went his way,
Light-hearted as he came;
And as he went half dead was ſhe
With anger and with ſhame.

The Love-Chace.

FOND Lover! pining night and day,
Come liſten to a hunter's lay;
The craft of each is to purſue,
Then learn from hunting how to woo.

It matters not to eager hound
The cover where the fox is found,
Whether he o'er the open fly,
Or echoing woods repeat his cry;
And when the welcome ſhout ſays "Gone!"
Then we, whate'er the line, ruſh on.
Seen ſeated in the banquet-hall,
Or view'd afoot at midnight ball,
Whene'er the beating of your heart
Proclaims a find, that moment ſtart!

If filence beft her humour fuit,
Then make at firft the running mute;
But if to mirth inclin'd, give tongue
In fpoken jeft or ditty fung;
Let laughter and light prattle cheer
The love-chace, when the maid is near;
When abfent, fancy muft purfue
Her form, and keep her face in view;
Fond thoughts muft like the bufy pack
Unceafingly her footfteps track.

The doubt, the agony, the fear,
Are fences raifed for you to clear;
Pufh on through pique, rebuff, and fcorn,
As hunters brufh through hedge of thorn;
On dark defpondency ftill look
As hunters on a yawning brook,
If for one moment on the brink
You falter, in you fall—and fink.

Though following faft the onward track,
Turn quickly when fhe doubles back;
Whenever check'd, whenever croft,
Still never deem the quarry loft;
Caft forward firft, if that fhould fail,
A backward caft may chance avail;
Caft far and near, caft all around,
Leave not untried one inch of ground.

Should envious rival at your fide
Cling, joftling as you onward ride,
Then let not jealoufy deter,
But ufe it rather as a fpur;
Outftrip him ere he interfere,
And fplafh the dirt in his career.

With other nymphs avoid all flirting,
Thofe hounds are hang'd that take to fkirting;
Of Cupid's angry lafh beware,
Provoke him not to cry " Ware hare;"
That winged whipper-in will rate
Your riot if you run not ftraight.

Though Reynard, with unwearied flight,
Should run from dawn till dufky night,
However fwift, however ftout,
Still perfeverance tires him out;
And never yet have I heard tell
Of maiden fo inflexible,
Of one caft in fo hard a mould,
So coy, fo ftubborn, or fo cold,
But courage, conftancy, and fkill
Could find a way to win her ftill;
Though at the find her timid cry
Be " No! no! no! indeed not I,"
The finifh ever ends in this,
Proud beauty caught, at laft fays, " Yes."

Hunters may range the country round,
And balk'd of fport no fox be found;
A blank the favourite gorfe may prove,
But maiden's heart, when drawn for love,
(Their gracious ftars let Lovers thank,)
Was ne'er, when drawn aright, drawn blank.

If any could, that Goddefs fair,
Diana, might have fcap'd the fnare;
That cunning huntrefs might have laugh'd,
If any could, at Cupid's fhaft;
Still, though reluctant to fubmit,
That tiny fhaft the Goddefs hit;
And on the mountain-top, they fay,
Endymion ftole her heart away.

Bear this in mind throughout the run,
"Faint heart fair lady never won;"
Thofe cravens are thrown out who fwerve,
"None but the brave the fair deferve."

Succefs will aye the Lover crown,
If guided by thefe rules laid down;
Then little Cupid, ftanding near,
Shall greet him with a lufty cheer;
And Hymen, that old huntfman, loop
The couples, while he fhouts, "Who-hoop!"

A Recollection.

I WELL remember in my youthful day,
   When firſt of love I felt the inward ſmart,
How one fair morning, eager all to ſtart,
My fellow hunters chided my delay.
I follow'd liſtleſs, for with tyrant ſway
   That ſecret grief oppreſs'd my aching heart,
   Till fond Hope whiſper'd, ere this day depart
Thy lov'd one thou ſhalt ſee—Away ! away !

The chace began, I ſhar'd its maddening glee,
   And rode amid the foremoſt in that run,
   Whoſe end, far diſtant, Love had well foretold.
Her dwelling lay betwixt my home and me ;
   We met, ſtill lingering ere it ſunk, the ſun
   O'erſpread her bluſhes with a veil of gold.

The Tantivy Trot.

I.

HERE'S to the old ones, of four-in-hand
      fame,
Harriſon, Peyton, and Ward, Sir ;
Here's to the faſt ones that after them came,
   Ford and the Lancaſhire Lord, Sir,
            Let the ſteam pot
            Hiſs till it's hot,
      Give me the ſpeed of the Tantivy Trot.

II.

Here's to the team, Sir, all harnefs'd to ftart,
　Brilliant in Brummagem leather ;
Here's to the waggoner, fkill'd in the art,
　Coupling the cattle together.
　　　　Let the fteam pot, &c.

III.

Here's to the dear little damfels within,
　Here's to the fwells on the top, Sir ;
Here's to the mufic in three feet of tin,
　And here's to the tapering crop, Sir.
　　　　Let the fteam pot, &c.

IV.

Here's to the fhape that is fhown the near fide,
　Here's to the blood on the off, Sir ;
Limbs with no check to their freedom of ftride !
Wind without whiftle or cough, Sir !
　　　　Let the fteam pot, &c.

V.

Here's to the arm that can hold 'em when gone,
　Still to a gallop inclin'd, Sir ;
Heads in the front with no bearing reins on !
　Tails with no cruppers behind, Sir !
　　　　Let the fteam pot, &c.

VI.

Here's to the dragſmen I've dragged into ſong,
    Saliſbury, Mountain, and Co., Sir;
Here's to the Cracknell who cracks them along
    Five twenty-fives at a go! Sir.
            Let the ſteam pot, &c.

VII.

Here's to Mac Adam the Mac of all Macs,
    Here's to the road we ne'er tire on;
Let me but roll o'er the granite he cracks,
    Ride ye who like it on iron.
            Let the ſteam pot
            Hiſs till it's hot,
    Give me the ſpeed of the Tantivy Trot.
1834.

Hawkſtone Bow-Meeting.

" Celeri certare ſagittâ
Invitat qui forte velint, et præmia ponit."
                                        ÆN. *lib.* v.

I.

FAREWELL to the Dane and the Weaver
    Farewell to the horn and the hound!
The Tarporley Swan, I muſt leave her
    Unſung till the ſeaſon come round;

My hunting whip hung in a corner,
  My bridle and faddle below,
I call on the Mufe and adorn her
  With baldrick, and quiver, and bow.

II.

Bright Goddefs ! affift me, recounting
  The names of toxophilites here,
How Watkin came down from the mountain,
  And Mainwaring up from the Mere ;
Affift me to fly with as many on
  As the fteed of Parnaflus can take,
Price, Parker, Lloyd, Kynafton, Kenyon,
  Dod, Cunliffe, Brooke, Owen and Drake.

III.

To witnefs the feats of the Bowmen,
  To ftare at the tent of the Bey,
Merrie Maidens and ale-drinking Yeomen
  At Hawkftone affemble to-day.
From the lord to the loweft in ftation,
  From the eaft of the fhire to the weft,
Salopia's whole population
  Within the green valley compreft.

IV.

In the hues of the target appearing,
  Now the bent of each archer is feen ;
The widow to *fable* adhering,
  The lover forfaken to *green ;*

For *gold* its affection difplaying,
   One fhaft at the centre is fped ;
Another a love tale betraying,
   Is aim'd with a blufh at the *red.*

v.

Pride pointing profanely at heaven,
   Humility fweeping the ground,
The arrow of gluttony driven
   Where ven'fon and fherry abound !
At *white* fee the maiden unmated
   The arrow of innocence draw,
While the fhaft of the matron is fated
   To faften its point in the *ftraw.*

vi.

Tell, fated with Geffler to grapple
   Till the tyrannous Bailiff was flain,
Let Switzerland boaft of the apple
   His arrow once fever'd in twain ;
We've an Eyton could prove to the Switzer,
   Such a feat were again to be done,
Should our hoft and his Lady think fit, Sir,
   To lend us the head of their fon !

vii.

The afh may be graceful and limber,
   The oak may be fturdy and true ;

You may fearch, but in vain, for a timber
  To rival the old Britifh yew!
You may roam through all lands, but there's no
    land
  Can fport fuch as Salop's afford,
And the Hill of all Hills is Sir Rowland!
  The hero of heroes my Lord!
    1835.

The Ball and the Battue.

I.

YE who care to encourage the long-feather'd
      breed,
To the Ball overnight let the Battue fucceed ;
      For when the heart aches,
      Ten to one the hand fhakes
  And fighs beget curfes, and curfes miftakes.

II.

For the fhot-belt of leather, in velveteen dreft,
I have doff'd the gold chain and laid by the filk
    veft,
      A pancake fo flat
      Was my ball-going hat,
  But a dumpling to fhoot in is better than that.

III.

My Manton to concert pitch tun'd for the day,
How the pheafants will reel in the air as I play!

While fnipes as they fly
Pirouette in the fky,
And rabbits and hares in the gallopade die.

IV.

" Once more might I view thee, fweet partner ! "
" Mark hare !
She is gone down the middle and up again
    there "—
        " That hand might I kifs,
        Mark cock !—did I mifs ?
Ye Gods, who could fhoot with a weapon
    like this ? "—

V.

In my breaft there's a thorn which no doctor can
    reach,
Ah me !—but what's this that I feel in my
    breech ?—
        Overwhelm'd by the pain
        Of a love that is vain—
How on earth fhall I ever get out of this drain ?

VI.

Thus a father may refcue his pheafants from
    flaughter,
The beft of prefervers his own pretty daughter ;

Sad thoughts in the pate,
On the heart a fad weight,
Who, blinded by Cupid, could ever aim
ftraight ?
1837.

On the Landlord

OF THE WHITE HORSE INN, AT ALPNACH,

IN SWITZERLAND.

I.

THE white horfe by mine hoft has been
brought to the poft,
Of his points and his pints he has reafon to boaft ;
To the guefts who approach him a welcome he
fnorts,
While they fill up his quarters and empty his
quarts.

II.

Neither weak in his *Hocks*, nor deficient in
Beaune,
In his *Cote* good condition though palpably fhown,
There are folk, not a few, who ftill call him a
fcrew ;
If applied to cork-drawing, the term may be true.

III.

Altogether reverfing the old-fafhion'd plan,
Here the horfe puts a bit in the mouth of the man ;
And fo long as not given to running away,
To the roadfter who enters he never fays
  " *Neigh.*"

IV.

He fets him, when caught, ftraight to work at
    the *Carte*,
With the coft of it faddles him ere he depart,
Gives him three feeds a day and the run of the
    bin,
And then makes him fork *out* for the good of
    the *Inn!*

V.

They may call the grey mare at his fide the beft
    horfe,
But they both pull together for better for worfe ;
Through the *heyday* of life may they pleafantly
    pafs,
Till by Death, that grim groom, they are turn'd
    out to grafs.

Cheſhire Chivalry.

On the 23rd of December, 1837, the Cheſhire Hounds found a fox in the plantation adjoining Tilſton Lodge. Running directly to the houſe, he baffled for a time all further purſuit by leaping through a window pane into the dairy. When captured, he was turned out at Wardle Gorſe, and after an unuſually quick burſt, in the courſe of which he croſſed two canals, was killed at Cholmondeſton.

I.

UNPUNISH'D ſhall Reynard our dairies attack,
His fate unrecorded in ſong?
Ah! no; when the captive was loos'd from a ſack,
There was not, fair milk-maid, a hound in the pack,
But was bent on avenging thy wrong.

II.

Would that thoſe who imagine all chivalry o'er,
Had encounter'd our gallant array;
Ne'er a hundred ſuch knights, e'en in ages of yore,
Took the field in the cauſe of one damſel before,
As were ſeen in the ſaddle that day.

III.

Their high-mettled courage no dangers appal,
So keen was the ardour diſplay'd;

Some lofe a frail ftirrup, fome flounder, fome fall,
Some gallantly ftem the deep waters, and all
　For the fake of the pretty milk-maid.

IV.

For thirty faft minutes Pug fled from his foes,
　Nor a moment for breathing allow'd;
When at Cholm'ftone the fkurry was brought to
　a clofe,
The nags that had follow'd him needed repofe,
　As their panting and fobbing avow'd.

V.

There, ftretch'd on the greenfward, lay Geoffry
　　the ftout,
　His heels were upturn'd to the fky,
From each boot flow'd a ftream, as it were from
　a fpout,
Away ftole the fox ere one half had run out,
　And away with frefh vigour we fly!

VI.

Once more to the water, though harafs'd and beat,
　The fox with a ftruggle fwam through;
Though the churn that he tainted fhall never be
　　fweet,
His heart's blood ere long fhall our vengeance
　　complete,
　And the caitiff his villany rue.

E

VII.

Stout Geoffry declar'd he would witnefs the kill
  Should he fwim in the faddle till dark;
Six horfemen undauntedly follow'd him ftill,
Till the fate that awaited the fteed of Sir Phil
  Put an end to this merry mud lark.

VIII.

Back, back, the bold Baronet roll'd from the fhore,
  Immers'd overhead in the wave;
The Tories 'gan think that the game was all o'er,
For their member was miffing a minute or more
  Ere he rofe from his watery grave.

IX.

Quoth Tollemache, more eager than all to make
    fail,
  (A foul that abhorreth reftraint,)
" Good doctor," quoth he, " fince thy remedies
    fail,
Since blifter, nor bleeding, nor pill-box avail,
  Cold bathing may fuit my complaint."

X.

When Williams paft o'er, at the burden they bore
  The waters all trembled with awe;
For the heaving canal, when it wafh'd him afhore,
Ne'er had felt fuch a fwell on its furface before,
  As the fwell from the Leamington Spa.

XI.

Harry Brooke, as a bird o'er the billow would fkim,
  Muft have flown to the furthermoft brink;
For the moifture had reach'd neither garment nor
  limb,
There was not a fpeck the boot polifh to dim,
  Nor a mudftain to tarnifh the pink.

XII.

The fox looking back, faw them fathom the tide,
  But was doom'd, ere they crofs'd it, to die;
Who-whoop may found fweeter by far on that fide,
But, thinks I to myfelf, I've a twenty-mile ride,
  And as yet my good leather is dry.

XIII.

Life-guardfman! why hang down in forrow thy
  head?
  Could our pack fuch a faft one outftrip?
Looking down at the ditch where his mare lay
  for dead,
"Pray, which way to Afton," he mournfully faid,
  And uptwifted the hair of his lip.

XIV.

Though of milk and of water I've made a long tale,
  When a livelier liquor's difplay'd,
I've a toaft that will fuit either claret or ale,
Good fport to the Kennel! fuccefs to the Pail!
  And a health to the pretty Milk-maid!
  1837.

On the *Picture* of the *Cheshire Hunt*,

PAINTED BY H. CALVERT IN 1840.

I.

ERE our Kennel a coal-hole envelop'd in
smoke,
Blood and bone shall give way to hot water and
coke ;
Make and shape, pace and pedigree, held as a jest,
All the power of the Stud in a copper comprest ;

II.

The green collar faded, good fellowship o'er,
Sir Peter and Barry remember'd no more,
From her Tarporley perch ere the Swan shall
drop down,
And her death-note be heard through the deso-
late town,

III.

Let Geoffrey record, in the reign of Queen Vic,
How the horse and his rider could still do the
trick ;
Let his journal, bequeath'd to posterity, show
How their sires rode a hunting in days long ago.

IV.

In colours unfading let Calvert design
A field not unworthy a sport so divine ;

For when Joe was their Huntfman, and Tom
    their firft Whip,
Who then could the chofen of Chefhire outftrip?

V.

Let the Laureate, ere yet he be laid on the fhelf,
Say how dearly he lov'd the diverfion himfelf;
How his Mufe o'er the field made each feafon a
    caft,
Gave a cheer to the foremoft, and rated the laft.

VI.

All the glories of Belvoir let Delamere tell,
And how Leicefterfhire griev'd when he bade
    them farewell;
Tell how oft with the Quorn he had liv'd through
    a burft
When the few were felected, the many difpers'd.

VII.

With fo graceful a feat, and with fpirits fo gay,
Let them learn from Sir Richard, erect on his
    grey,
How the beft of all cures for a pain in the back
Is to fit on the pigfkin and follow the pack.

VIII.

Say, Glegg, how the chace requir'd judgment and
    fkill,
How to coax a tir'd horfe over valley and hill;

How his fhoe fhould be fhap'd, how to nurfe him
  when fick,
And when out how to fpare him by making a
  nick.

IX.

Charley Cholmondeley, make known how, in
  Wellefley's campaign
When the mail arriv'd loaded with laurels from
  Spain,
How cheers through the club-room were heard
  to refound,
While, upfill'd to the brim, the Quafitum went
  round.

X.

Let Wickfted defcribe and futurity learn
All the points of a hound, from the nofe to the
  ftern ;
He whofe joy 'tis to dance, without fiddle or pipe,
To the tune of Who-whoop with a fox in his gripe,

XI.

Say, Dorfold's black Squire, how, when trundling
  ahead,
Ever clofe to your fide clung the Colonel in red ;
He who, charge what he would, never came to a
  hitch,
A fence or a Frenchman, it matter'd not which.

XII.

Let Cornwall declare, though a long abfentee,
With what pain and what grief he deferted High
    Legh ;
How he car'd not to prance on the Corfo at Rome,
While fuch fport Winterbottom afforded at home.

XIII.

The rules of hard riding let Tollemache impart,
How to lean o'er the pommel and dafh at a ftart ;
Emerging at once from a crowd in fufpenfe,
How in fafety he rides who is firft at the fence.

XIV.

How with caution 'tis pleafanter far to advance
Let them learn from De Tabley, Tom Tatton
    and France ;
· Who void of ambition ftill follow the chace,
Nor think that all fport is dependent on pace.

XV.

Twin managers ! tell them, Smith Barry from
    Cork,
And Dixon, who ftudied the fcience in York,
Though we boaft but one neck to our Tarporley
    Swan,
Two heads in the kennel are better than one.

XVI.

Let Entwiftle, Blackburne, and Trafford difown
Thofe Lancafhire flats, where the fport was un-
    known ;

Releas'd from St. Stephen's let Patten declare
How fox-hunting folac'd a fenator's care.

XVII.

Let the bones of the fteed which Sir Philip be-
    ftrode
'Mid the foffils at Oulton be carefully ftow'd ;
For the animal foon, whether hunter or war-horfe,
Will be rare in the land as an Ichthyofaurus.

XVIII.

Still diftant the day, yet in ages to come,
When the gorfe is uprooted, the fox-hound is
    dumb,
May verfe make immortal the deeds of the field,
And the fhape of each fteed be on canvas reveal'd.

XIX.

Let the pencil be dipt in the hues of the chace,
Contentment and health be pourtray'd in each
    face ;
Let the foreground difplay the felect of the pack,
And Chefter's green vale be outftretch'd in the
    back !

XX.

When the time-honour'd race of our gentry fhall
    end,
The poor no protector, the farmer no friend,

They fhall here view the face of the old Tatton
    Squire,
And regret the paft fport that once gladden'd our
    Shire.

The Breeches.

I.

WHEN I mention the " Breeches," I feel
    no remorfe,
For the ladies all know 'tis an evergreen gorfe ;
They are not of leather, they are not of plufh,
But expreffly cut out for Joe maiden to brufh.

II.

Good luck to the 'prentice by whom they were
    made !
His fhears were a ploughfhare, his needle a fpade ;
May each landlord a pair to this pattern befpeak,
The Breeches that lafted us three days a week.

III.

The fox is away and Squire Royds made it known,
Setting ftraightway to work at a pace of his own ;
Paft him fped Tollemache, as inftant in flight
As a ftar when it fhoots through the azure of
    night.

IV.

They who witnefs'd the pack as it fkirted the Spa,
By the head they then carried a ftruggle forefaw;
At their heels a white horfe with his head in the
    air,
But his bridle was loofe, and his faddle was bare.

V.

May Peel (near the Breeches at ftarting o'er-
    thrown,
Where he left the impreffion in mud of his
    own;)
When next he thinks fit this white horfe to be-
    ftraddle,
See lefs of the Breeches and more of the faddle.

VI.

From Spurftow we pointed towards Bunbury
    Church,
Some rounding that cover were left in the lurch;
By Hurlefton we hurried, nor e'er tighten'd rein,
Till check'd for one moment in Baddiley lane.

VII.

When we pafs'd the old gorfe and the meadows
    beneath,
When, acrofs the canal, we approach'd Afton
    Heath,

There were riders who took to the water like rats,
There were fteeds without horfemen, and men
    without hats.

VIII.

How many came down to the Edleftone brook,
How many came down, not to leap—but to look;
The fteeds that ftood ftill with a ftitch in their
    fide,   .
Will remember the day when the Breeches were
    tried. .

IX.

The pack, prefling onwards, ftill merrily went,
Till at Dorfold they needed no longer a fcent;
Man and maid rufhing forth ftood aloft on the
    wall,
And uprais'd a view hollo that fhook the old hall.

X.

Too weak for the open, too hot for the drain,
He crofs'd and recrofs'd Ran'moor covers in vain;
When he reach'd the Bull's wood, he lay down
    in defpair,
And we hollow'd whó-hoop, as they worried him
    ,there.

XI.

Pufs in boots is a fable to children well known,
The Dog in a doublet at Sandon is fhown,
Henceforth when a landlord good liquor can boaft,
Let the Fox and the Breeches be hung on his poft.

XII.

From Vulpecide villains our foxes fecure,
May thefe evergreen Breeches till doomfday en-
    dure !
Go ! all ye good fquires, if my ditty fhould pleafe,
Go clothe your bare acres in Breeches like thefe.
   1841.

Infcription on the Handle of a Fox's Brufh,
  mounted and prefented by the Author
    to Wilbraham Tollemache, Efq.
      Feb. 20, 1841.

WE found our fox at Brindley; thrice that
    week
The gorfe was drawn, and thrice with like fuccefs.
For nigh two hours, o'er many a mile of grafs,
We chas'd him thence to Dorfold, where he died.
Tollemache ! in admiration of thy fkill'd
And gallant riding to the pack that day,
To thee I yield the Brufh, efteem not thou
The trophy lefs thus proffer'd by a friend.

The Sawyer.

THE imaginary cataftrophe, which is the fubject of the following lines, originated in the warning given by one of our party to the Factor at Abergeldie, that, if he perfifted in felling timber during the term of our leafe, he muft hold himfelf relponfible fhould any one "fhoot a Sawyer."

I.

NOW Abergeldie gillies, as they range our
        foreft-ground,
See fawing here, fee fawing there, fee fawpits all
        around;
In fear and dread, as on they tread no whifky
        dare they touch,
No! not a drop, left, neck and crop, they take a
        drop too much.

II.

" Aim ftraight to-day, my comrades, 'twill be
        truly a dear hit
If, fhooting deer in the foreft here, manflaughter
        you commit ;
If feller, fell'd, fhould in the act of ftriking be
        down ftruck,
Or Sawyer kick the bucket here, miftaken for a
        Buck."

III.

Vain words ! forth came a bounding ftag, his
    antler'd head on high,
And, caring not a whiftle for the balls that
    whiftled by,
Away, alive and kicking, to the diftant mountain
    fped ;—
Though de'il a bit the deer was hit, the deal-
    cutter was dead.

IV.

His fkull was crack'd, his only wage that day was
    half-a-crown,
He was cutting up a billet when the bullet cut
    him down ;
Many thoufand feet of timber had that Sawyer
    rent in twain,
Now himfelf was fplit afunder, very much againft
    the grain.

V.

We needed not the Sexton with his pickaxe and
    his fpade
In the fawpit which himfelf had dug his grave was
    ready made ;
Top Sawyer though he had been, to the bottom
    he was thruft,
And we binn'd him like a bottle of old Sherry in
    fawduft.

VI.

Full many a railway sleeper had he made since
  peep of day,
Ere night himself a sleeper in his narrow bed he
  lay;
No tear-drop unavailingly we shed upon the
  spot,
But we sprinkled him with whisky to preserve
  him from dry rot.

VII.

Oh no! we never mention him, that shot we
  never own,
We book'd him in the game book as an "animal
  unknown!"
We know not how the wife and bairns without
  his board subsist,
We only know we hit him, and he has not
  since been miss'd.

1844.

Song, written for and fung by

I. H. SMITH BARRY, ESQ.

OWNER OF THE "COLUMBINE" YACHT, WHEN

PRESIDENT OF THE TARPORLEY

HUNT MEETING, 1845.

I.

NOW riding fafe at anchor, idly floats the
"Columbine,"
And the perils of the ocean in November I refign;
With other meffmates round me, merry comrades
every one,
To-night I take command, boys, of the gallant
fhip, the "Swan."

Chorus.

Then up, boys! up for action, with a hearty three
times three,
What tars are half fo jolly as the tars of Tarporley?

II.

'Tis true, though ftrange, this gallant fhip in
water cannot fwim,
A fea of rofy wine, boys, is the fea fhe loves to fkim;
The billows of that red fea are in bumpers tofs'd
about,
Our fpirits rifing higher as the tide is running out!
Chorus.

III.

Still fwinging at her moorings, with a cable round
   her neck,
Though long as fummer lafteth all deferted is her
   deck,
She fcuds before the breezes of November faft
   and free,
O ! ne'er may fhe be ftranded in the ftraits of
   Tarporley.
                                    Chorus.

IV.

By adverfe gale or hurricane her fails are never
   rent,
H canvas fwells with laughter, and her freight
   is merriment ;
The lightning on her deck, boys, is the lightning
   flafh of wit,
Loud cheers in thunder rolling till her very
   timbers fplit !
                                    Chorus.

V.

We need not Archimedes with his fcrew on board
   the Swan,
The fcrew that draws the cork, boys, is the
   fcrew that drives us on,
And fhould we be becalm'd, boys, while giving
   chafe to care,

F

When the brimming bowl is heated we have
ſteam in plenty there.

Chorus.

VI.

No rocks have we to ſplit on, no foes have we to
fight,
No dangers to alarm us, while we keep the
reckoning right;
We fling the gold about, boys, though we never
heave the lead,
And long as we can raiſe the wind our courſe is
ſtraight a-head.

Chorus.

VII.

The index of our compaſs is the bottle that we
trowl,
To the chair again revolving like the needle to
the pole;
The motto on our glaſſes is to us a fixed ſtar,
We know while we can ſee it, boys, exactly
where we are.

Chorus.

VIII.

To their ſweethearts let our bachelors a ſparkling
bumper fill,
To their wives let thoſe who have 'em fill a
fuller bumper ſtill;

O ! never while we've health, boys, may we
    quit this gallant fhip,
But every year, together here, enjoy this pleafure
    trip.
                    Chorus.

IX.

Behind me ftands my anceftor, Sir Peter ftands
    before,
Two pilots who have weather'd many a ftormy
    night of yore ;
So may our fons and grandfons, when we are
    dead and gone,
Spend many a merry night, boys, in the cabin of
    the Swan.

                    Chorus.
Then up, boys ! up for action, with a hearty
    three times three,
What tars are half fo jolly as the tars of
    Tarporley ?
1845.

Tarwood.

A RUN WITH THE HEYTHROP.

H E waited not—he was not found—
    No warning note from eager hound,
But echo of the diftant horn,

From outſkirts of the covert borne,
Where Jack the Whip in ambuſh lay,
Proclaim'd that he was gone away.

Away! ere yet that blaſt was blown,
The fox had o'er the meadow flown;
Away! away! his flight he took,
Straight pointing for the Windruſh brook!

The Miller, when he heard the pack,
Stood tiptoe on his loaded ſack,
He view'd the fox acroſs the flat,
And, needleſs ſignal, wav'd his hat;
He ſaw him clear with eaſy ſtride
The ſtream by which the mill was plied;
Like phantom fox he ſeem'd to fly,
With ſpeed unearthly flitting by.

The road that leads to Witney town,
He travell'd neither up nor down;
But ſtraight away, like arrow ſped
From cloth-yard bow, he ſhot a-head.
Now Cokethorpe on his left he paſt,
Now Ducklington behind him caſt,
Now by Bampton, now by Lew,
Now by Clanfield, on he flew;
At Grafton now his courſe inclin'd,
And Kelmſcote now is left behind!

Where waters of the Ifis lave
The meadows with its claffic wave,
O'er thofe meadows fpeeding on,
He near'd the bridgeway of St. John ;
He paufed a moment on the bank,
His footfteps in the ripple fand,
He felt how cold, he faw how ftrong
The rapid river roll'd along ;
Then turn'd away, as if to fay,
" All thofe who like to crofs it may."

The Huntfman, though he view'd him back,
View'd him too late to turn the pack,
W██h o'er the tainted meadow preft,
An██each'd the river all abreaft ;
In with one plunge, one billowy fplafh,
In—altogether—in they dafh,
Together ftem the wintry tide,
Then fhake themfelves on t'other fide !
" Hark, hollo back !" that loud halloo
Then eager, and more eager grew,
Till every hound, recroffing o'er,
Stoop'd forward to the fcent once more ;
Nor further aid, throughout the day,
From Huntfman or from Whip had they.

Away ! away ! uncheck'd in pace,
O'er grafs and fallow fwept the chace ;
To hounds, to horfes, or to men,

No child's play was the ſtruggle then ;
A trefpaſſer on Milward's ground,
He climb'd the pale that fenc'd it round ;
Then cloſe by Little Hemel ſped,
To Fairford pointing ſtraight a-head,
Though now, the pack approaching nigh,
He heard his death-note in the cry.
They view'd him, and then ſeem'd their race
The very lightning of the chace !
The fox had reach'd the Southropp lane,
He ſtrove to crofs it, but in vain,
The pack roll'd o'er him in his ſtride,
And onward ſtruggling ſtill—he died.

This gallant fox, in Tarwood found,
Had crofs'd full twenty miles of ground ;
Had fought in cover, left or right,
No ſhelter to conceal his flight ;
But nigh two hours the open kept,
As ſtout a fox as ever ſtept !
That morning, in the faddle ſet,
A hundred men at Tarwood met ;
The eager ſteeds which they beſtrode
Pac'd to and fro the Witney road,
For hard as iron ſhoe that trod
Its ſurface, the unyielding ſod ;
Till midday ſun had thaw'd the ground
And made it fit for foot of hound,

They champ'd the bit and twitch'd the rein,
And paw'd the frozen earth in vain,
Impatient with fleet hoof to fcour
The vale, each minute feem'd an hour;
Still Rumour fays of that array
Scarce ten liv'd fairly through the day.

Ah! how fhall I in fong declare
The riders who were foremoft there?
A fit excufe how fhall I find
For every rider left behind?

Though Cokethorpe feem one open plain,
'Tis flafh'd and fluic'd with many a drain,
And he who clears thofe ditches wide
Muft needs a goodly fteed beftride.
From Bampton to the river's bounds
The race was run o'er pafture grounds;
Yet many a horfe of blood and bone
Was heard to crofs it with a groan;
For blackthorns ftiff the fields divide
With watery ditch on either fide.
By Lechlade's village fences rife
Of every fort and every fize,
And frequent there the grievous fall
O'er flippery bank and crumbling wall;
Some planted deep in cornfield ftand,
A fix'd incumbrance on the land!

While others prove o'er poſt and rail
The merits of the ſliding ſcale.

Ah ! much it grieves the Muſe to tell
At Clanfield how Valentia fell ;
He went, they ſay, like one bewitch'd,
Till headlong from the ſaddle pitch'd ;
There, recklefs of the pain, he ſigh'd
To think he might not onward ride ;
Though fallen from his pride of place,
His heart was following ſtill the chace ;
He bade his many friends forbear
The proffer'd aid, nor tarry there ;
" O ! heed me not, but ride away !
The Tarwood fox muſt die to-day ! "

Nor fell Valentia there alone,
There too in mid career was thrown
The Huntſman—in the breaſtplate ſwung
His heels—his body earthward hung ;
With many a tug at neck and mane,
Struggling he reach'd his ſeat again ;
Once more upon the back of Spangle,
His head and heels at proper angle,
(Poor Spangle in a piteous plight,)
He look'd around him, bolt upright,
Nor near nor far could ſuccour ſee,—
Where can the faithlefs Juliet be ?
He would have given half his wage

Juft then to fee her on the ftage;
The pack thofe meads by Ifis bound
Had reach'd ere Jem his Juliet found;
Well thence with fuch a prompter's aid,
Till Reynard's death her part fhe play'd.

There Ifaac from the chace withdrew,
(A horfe is Ifaac, not a Jew,)
Outftretch'd his legs, and fhook his back,
Right glad to be reliev'd of Jack;
And Jack, right glad his back to quit,
Gave Beatrice a benefit.

Moifture and mud the " Fungus " fuit,
In boggy ditch he, taking root,
For minutes ten or thereabout,
Stood planted, till they pluck'd him out.
By application of fpur rowel
Charles rubb'd him dry without a towel.

Say, as the pack by Kelmfcote fped,
Say who thofe horfemen cloth'd in red?
Spectators of the chace below,
Themfelves no fign of movement fhow;
No wonder—they were all aghaft
To fee the pace at which it paft;
The " White Horfe Vale "—well known to Fame
The pack to which it gives a name;

And there they ftood as if fpell bound,
Their morning fox as yet unfound;
Borne from that wood, their huntfman's cheer
Drew many a Tarwood ftraggler near,
And he who felt the pace too hot,
There gladly fought a refting fpot;
Himfelf of that White Horfe availing,
When confcious that his own was failing.

Thus fhips, when they no more can bide
The fury of the wind and tide,
If chance fome tranquil port they fpy,
Where veffels fafely fhelter'd lie,
There feek a refuge from the gale,
Caft anchor, and let down the fail.

The fpeed of horfe, the pluck of man,
They needed both, who led the van;
This Holmes can tell, who through the day
Was ever foremoft in the fray;
And Holloway, with beft intent,
Still fhivering timber as he went;
And Williams, clinging to the pack
As if the League were at his back;
And Tollit, ready ftill to fell
The nag that carried him fo well.

A pretty fight at firft to fee
Young Pretyman on Modefty!

But Pretyman went on fo faft,
That Modefty took fright at laft ;
So bent was fhe to fhun difgrace,
That in the brook fhe hid her face ;
So bafhful, that to drag her out
They fetch'd a team and tackle ftout.

When younger men of lighter weight
Some tale of future fport relate,
Let Whippy fhow the brufh he won,
And tell them of the Tarwood run ;
While Rival's portrait, on the wall,
Shall oft to memory recall
The gallant fox, the burning fcent,
The leaps they leapt, the pace they went ;
How *Whimfey* led the pack at firft,
When Reynard from the woodfide burft ;
How *Pamela*, a puppy hound,
Firft feiz'd him, ftruggling on the ground ;
How *Prudence* fhunn'd the taint of hare,
Taught young in life to have a care ;
How *Alderman*, a foxhound ftaunch,
Worked well upon an empty paunch ;
How Squires were, following thee, upfet,
Right honourable *Baronet ;*
How, as the pack by Lechlade flew,
Where clofe and thick the fences grew,
Three Bitches led the tuneful throng,

All worthy of a place in fong;
Old *Fairplay*, ne'er at fkirting caught,
And *Penfive* fpeeding quick as thought;
While *Handfome* prov'd the adage true,
They handfome are that handfome do!

Then long may courteous Redefdale live!
And oft his pack fuch gallops give!
Should fox again fo ftoutly run,
May I be there and fee the fun!
1845.

A " Meet " at the Hall, and a " Find " in the Wood.

I.

THE wind in the fouth, and the firft faint
blufhes
Of morn amid clouds difpers'd,
As a ftream in its ftrength through a floodgate
rufhes,
The hounds from their kennel burft.

II.

The huntfman is up on his favourite bay,
The whips are all aftride,
Leifurely trotting their onward way
To the diftant cover fide.

III.

Sweetly the blackbird, and fweetly the thrufh,
  Greeting them, feem to fay,
In the chorus that rings from each hawthorn bufh,
  " Good fport to the pack to-day."

IV.

Lads from the village now after them race,
  Afking with eager fhout,
And ruddy with joy at the thoughts of a chace,
  " Where do the hounds turn out ?"

V.

Now mafking the flope with its dufky fcreen,
  A wood in front appears,
And a Hall high-gabled the glittering fheen
  Of its vane-deck'd turret rears.

VI.

The chimney-fhafts, wreathed with fmoke, be-
    token
  Full many a gueft within,
While words of welcome in honefty fpoken
  The heart of each ftranger win.

VII.

A white hand unlatches her cafement bar ;
  A murmur of joy refounds :

They're coming! they're coming! fee, yonder
   they are !
They're coming! the hounds! the hounds!

VIII.

A cloud, fo it feem'd, might have dropp'd from
   the fky
When the fun was in the weft,
To clothe with a mantle of crimfon dye
The lawn by thofe riders preft.

IX.

Steadily, fteadily, to and fro,
   Old hunters pace the ground ;
Heads high in air the young ones throw,
   Pawing and plunging round.

X.

See ! to unkennel a noifier pack,
   The fchool-gate open flung,
By the defk-weary pedant, whofe heart leaps back
   To the day when himfelf was young.

XI.

Dreft in the pride of her Sunday array,
   The hufwife ftands aloof,
Timidly plucking her child away
   From the lunge of uplifted hoof.

XII.

Curb'd for that hand which the casement unbarr'd,
  To the porch is a palfrey led,
The trim gravel court by the prancing scarr'd
  Of his proud and impatient tread ;

XIII.

A fair-hair'd youth to the portal flew,
  And stood by her bridle-rein ;
He lifts her light foot to the stirrup-shoe,
  And they follow the hunting-train.

XIV.

His saddle-bow hung with a silver horn,
  All eyes on the master gaze,
Lord of the hunting-field ! monarch, this morn,
  Of all that he surveys !

XV.

The Huntsman has drunk to the health of the
      Squire
From the depth of the leathern jack,
And lifting his cap, as the gentry admire
  His well-condition'd pack,

XVI.

He speeds, with sure hope, to the cover hard by—
  Streaking the greenwood now,
Red coats bright with the berries vie
  That hang on the holly bough.

XVII.

Hark ! from the cover a fox halloo'd ;
  The hounds to the open fly ;
Horfes and men, as they crafh through the wood,
  Made mad by the merry cry.

XVIII.

Fainter and fainter in diftance died
  The tumult of the chace ;
Till filent as death was the green hill-fide,
  The Hall a deferted place.

XIX.

I follow them not ; the good fox they found
  Sped many a mile away ;
That run was the talk of the country round
  For many an after day.

XX.

The brufh by that youth who had ridden hard,
  Brought home in the twilight hour,
A gift for the hand which the cafement unbarr'd,
  Was hung in the maiden's bower.

Song.

I.

STAGS in the foreſt lie, hares in the valley-o!
  Web-footed otters are ſpear'd in the lochs;
Beaſts of the chace that are not worth a Tally-ho!
All are ſurpaſs'd by the gorſe-cover fox!
        Fiſhing, though pleaſant,
        I ſing not at preſent,
        Nor ſhooting the pheaſant,
            Nor fighting of cocks;
        Song ſhall declare a way
        How to drive care away,
        Pain and deſpair away,
            Hunting the fox!

II.

Bulls in gay Seville are led forth to ſlaughter, nor
  Dames, in high rapture, the ſpectacle ſhocks;
Brighter in Britain the charms of each daughter,
      nor
Dreads the bright charmer to follow the fox.
        Spain may delight in
        A ſport ſo exciting;
        Whilſt 'ſtead of bull-fighting
            We fatten the ox;
        Song ſhall declare a way, &c.

G

III.

England's green paftures are graz'd in fecurity,
    Thanks to the Saxon who car'd for our flocks!
He who referving the fport for futurity,
    Sweeping our wolves away left us the fox.
        When joviality
        Chafes formality,
        When hofpitality
            Cellars unlocks;
        Song fhall declare a way
        How to drive care away,
        Pain and defpair away,
            Hunting the fox!

Sport in the Highlands.

WRITTEN AT TOLLY HOUSE IN ROSS-SHIRE.

I.

UP in the morning! the river runs merrily,
    Clouds are above and the breezes blow
      cool,
Tie the choice fly now, and cafting it warily,
    Fifh the dark ripple that curls o'er the pool;

Steadily play with him,
On through the fpray with him,
Gaff, and away with him
    On to the fhore !
Paftime at Tolly now,
Oh ! it is jolly now,
Sad melancholy now
    Haunts us no more !

II.

Up in the morning ! young birds in full feather
    now,
Brood above brood on the mountain fide lie ;
Setters well broken are ranging the heather now,
    Bird after bird taking wing but to die !
        Home then to number
        The groufe that encumber
        Our gillies, where flumber
          To toil gives relief.
        Paftime at Tolly now,
        Oh ! it is jolly now,
        No melancholy now,
          Sorrow, or grief.

III.

Up ! up ! at peep-o-day, clad for a tuffle now !—
    Keen eyes have mark'd the wild hart on the
    hill ;

Toil for the ftalker!—wind, finew and mufcle,
  now
All will be needed, ere tefting his fkill!
        Gillies now frolicking,
        Roaring and rollicking,
        Hey! for a grollocking,—
            Rip up the deer,
        Paftime at Tolly now,
        Oh! it is jolly now,
        No melancholy now
            Haunteth us here.

                    IV.

Up! up! at peep-o-day; what may your pleafure
  be?
Black-cock or ptarmigan, roebuck or hare?
Bright with delight let each moment of leifure be,
  Left in the lowlands, a fig for dull care!
        Wood, ftream, and heather now,
        Yielding together now,
        Sport for all weather now,—
            Up in the morn!
        Paftime at Tolly now,
        Oh! it is jolly now,
        Sad melancholy, now
            Laugh her to fcorn!
    1845.

" Importation of Vermin."

" A STEAM fhip arrived yefterday from Boulogne with a
cage of live foxes, configned to order."—*Daily News,*
Feb. 1ft, 1848, at which time there was much talk of the
poffibility of a French invafion.

I.

" I MPORTED Vermin:"—fay, thou fcribbler,
when
Thofe fiercer vermin on our coaft alight,
Who bark with drumftick and with bayonet bite,
As daily threat thy brethren of the pen ;
When England fummons her true-hearted men,
(Whether invader to the chace invite
With foes or foxes, putting both to flight,)
Say, of thefe twain which beft will ferve her then.

The joyous hunter, he who cheers the pack,
His fleet fteed urging over vale and hill,
Who fhuns no hardfhip and who knows no fear,

Or he, who bending o'er the defk his back,
In gas-lit office drives the flippant quill,
And talks of " vermin imports " with a fneer ?

Bowmeeting Song.

ARLEY HALL, SEPTEMBER 4, 1851.

I.

THE tent is pitch'd, the target rear'd, the
ground is meafured out,
For the weak arm fixty paces, and one hundred
for the ftout !
Come, gather ye together then, the youthful and
the fair,
And poet's lay, to future day, the victor fhall
declare !

II.

Let bufy fingers lay afide the needle and the thread,
To prick the golden canvas with a pointed arrow-
head ;
Ye fportfmen quit the ftubble, quit, ye fifhermen,
the ftream,
Fame and glory ftand before you, brilliant eyes
around you beam.

III.

All honour to the long-bow which many a battle
won,
Ere powder blaz'd and bullet flew, from arquebus
or gun ;

All honour to the long-bow, which merry men of
    yore,
With hound and horn at early morn, in greenwood
    foreſt bore.

IV.

O ! famous is the archer's ſport, 'twas honour'd
    long ago,
The God of Love, the God of Wit, bore both of
    them a bow;
Love laughs to-day in beauty's eye and bluſhes on
    her cheek,
And wit is heard in every word, that merry
    archers ſpeak;

V.

The archer's heart, though, like his bow, a tough
    and ſturdy thing,
Is pliant ſtill and yielding, when affeċtion pulls
    the ſtring;
All his words and all his aċtions are like arrows,
    pointed well
To hit that golden centre, where true love and
    friendſhip dwell.

VI.

They tell us in that outline which the lips of
    beauty ſhow,
How Cupid found a model for his heart-ſubduing
    bow;

The arrows in his quiver are the glances from her
    eye,   .
A feather from love's wing it is, that makes the
    arrow fly !

Farmer Dobbin.

A DAY WI' THE CHESHUR FOX DUGS.

I.

"OULD mon, it's welly milkin toim, where
    ever 'aft 'ee bin ?
Thear's flutch upo' thoi coat, oi fee, and blood
    upo' thoi chin ;"
" Oiv bin to fee the gentlefolk o' Chefhur roid a
    run ;
Owd wench ! oiv been a hunting, an oiv feen
    fome rattling fun.

II.

" Th' owd mare was i' the fmithy when the
    huntfman, he trots through,
Black Bill agate o' ammering the laft nail in her
    fhoe ;
The cuvver laid fo wheam loik, an fo jovial foin
    the day,
Says I, ' Owd mare, we'll tak a fling and fee 'em
    go away.'

III.

" When up, an oi'd got ſhut ov aw the hackney
    pads an traps,
Orſe dealers an orſe jockey lads, and ſuch loik
    ſwaggering chaps,
Then what a power o' gentlefolk did I ſet oies
    upon !
A reining in their hunters, aw blood orſes every
    one !

IV.

" They'd aw got bookſkin leathers on, a fitten
    'em ſo toight,
As roind an plump as turmits be, an juſt about
    as whoit ;
Their ſpurs wor maid o' ſiller, and their buttons
    maid o' braſs,
Their coats wor red as carrots an their collurs
    green as graſs.

V.

" A varment looking gemman on a woiry tit I
    feed,
An another cloſe befoid him, ſitting noble on his
    ſteed ;
They ca' them both owd codgers, but as freſh as
    paint they look,
John Glegg, Eſquoir, o' Withington, an bowd
    Sir Richard Brooke.

VI.

"I feed Squoir Geffrey Shakerley, the beft un o'
    that breed,
His fmoiling feace tould plainly how the fport wi'
    him agreed;
I feed the 'Arl ov Grofvenor, a loikly lad to roid,
I feed a foight worth aw the reft, his farencly
    young broid.

VII.

"Zur Umferry de Trafford an the Squoir ov
    Arley Haw,
His pocket full o' rigmarole, a rhoiming on 'em
    aw;
Two Members for the Cointy, both aloik ca'd
    Egerton;—
Squoir Henry Brooks and Tummus Brooks,
    they'd aw green collurs on.

VIII.

"Eh! what a mon be Dixon John, ov Aftle
    Haw, Efquoir,
You wudna foind, and meafure him, his marrow
    in the fhoir;
Squoir Wilbraham o' the Foreft, death and danger
    he defoies,
When his coat be toightly button'd up, and fhut
    be both his oies.

IX.

" The Honerable Lazzles, who from forrin parts
 be cum,
An a chip of owd Lord Delamere, the Honerable
 Tum ;
Squoir Fox an Booth an Worthington, Squoir
 Maffey an Squoir Harne,
An many more big fportfmen, but their neames
 I didna larn.

X.

" I feed that great commander in the faddle,
 Captain Whoit,
An the pack as thrung'd about him was indeed a
 gradely foight ;
The dugs look'd foin as fatin, an himfel look'd
 hard as nails,
An he giv the fwells a caution not to roid upo'
 their tails.

XI.

" Says he, ' Young men o' Monchefter an
 Livverpoo, cum near,
Oiv juft a word, a warning word, to whifper in
 your ear,
When, ftarting from the cuvver foid, ye fee bowd
 Reynard burft,
We canna 'ave no 'unting if the gemmen go it
 firft.'

XII.

" Tom Rance has got a fingle oie, wurth many
  another's two,
He held his cap abuv his yed to fhow he'd had a
  view ;
Tom's voice was loik th' owd raven's when he
  fkroik'd out ' Tally-ho ! '
For when the fox had feen Tom's feace he thoght
  it toim to go.

XIII.

"Ey moy ! a pratty jingle then went ringin through
  the fkoy,
Furft Victory, then Villager begun the merry
  croy,
Then every maith was open from the oud'un to
  the pup,
An aw the pack together took the fwellin chorus
  up.

XIV.

" Eh moy ! a pratty fkouver then was kick'd up
  in the vale,
They fkim'd acrofs the running brook, they topp'd
  the poft an rail,
They didna ftop for razzur cop, but play'd at
  touch an go,
An them as mifs'd a footin there lay doubled up
  below.

XV.

" I feed the 'ounds a croffing Farmer Flareup's
  boundary loin,
Whofe daughter plays the peany an drinks whoit
  fherry woin,
Gowd rings upon her finger and filk ftockings on
  her feet ;
Says I, ' it won't do him no harm to roid acrofs
  his wheat.'

XVI.

" So, toightly houdin on by'th yed, I hits th'owd
  mare a whop,
Hoo plumps into the middle o' the wheatfield neck
  an crop ;
And when hoo floinder'd out on it I catch'd another
  fpin,
An, miffis, that's the cagion o' the blood upo' my
  chin.

XVII.

" I never ofs'd another lep, but kep the lane, an
  then
In twenty minutes' toim about they turn'd toart
  me agen ;
The fox was foinly daggled, an the tits aw out
  o' breath,
When they kilt him in the open, an owd Dobbin
  feed the death.

XVIII.

" Loik dangling of a babby, then the Huntfman
    hove him up,
The dugs a bayin roind him, while the gemman
    croid, ' Whoo-hup ! '
As doefome cawves lick fleetings out o' th' piggin
    in the fhed,
They worried every inch of him, aw but his tail
    an yed.

XIX.

" Now, miffis, fin the markets be a doing moderate
    well,
Oiv welly maid my moind up juft to buoy a nag
    myfel ;
For to keep a farmer's fpirits up 'gen things be
    gettin low,
Theer's nothin loik Fox-huntin and a rattling
    Tally-ho ! "

  1853.

The Blooming Evergreen.

I.

ERE the adventurers, nicknamed Plantagenet,
    Buckled the helm on, their foes to difmay,
They pluck'd a broom-fprig which they wore as
    a badge in it,
Meaning thereby they would fweep them away.

Long the genifta fhall flourifh in ftory,
  Green as the laurels their chivalry won;
As the broom-fprig excited thofe heroes to glory,
  May the gorfe-plant encourage our foxes to
    run.

II.

Held by Diana in due eftimation,
  Bedeck with a gorfe-flower the goddefs's fhrine;
Throughout the wide range of this blooming
    creation,
  It has but one rival, and that one the vine.
Pluck me then, Bacchus, a clufter and, fqueezing
    it,
  Pour the red juice till the goblet o'erflows;
Then in the joy of my heart, will I, feizing it,
  Drink to the land where this Evergreen grows.

Chefhire Jumpers.

I.

I ASK'D in much amazement, as I took my
    morning ride,
"What means this monfter meeting, that colleẟts
    at Highwayfide?
Who are ye? and what ftrange event this gather-
    ing crowd excites?
Are ye fcarlet men of Babylon, or mounted Mor-
    monites?"

II.

A bearded man on horfeback anfwered blandly
    with a fmile,—
" Good Sir, no Canters are we, though we canter
    many a mile ;
Nor will you find a Ranter here amongft our
    merry crew,
Though if you feek a Roarer, there may chance
    be one or two.

III.

" With Shakers and with Quakers no connection
    Sir, have we ;
We are not Plymouth Brothers, Chefhire Jumpers
    though we be ;
'Tis mine between two champions bold to judge,
    if judge I can,
And fettle which, o'er hedge and ditch, will prove
    the better man.

IV.

" Mark well thefe two conditions, he who falls
    upon the field,
Or he whofe horfe refufes twice, the victory muft
    yield."
As thus he fpake he ftrok'd his beard, and bade
    the champions go ;
His beard was black as charcoal, but their faces
    white as fnow.

V.

The ladies wave their kerchiefs as the rival
    jumpers ſtart,
A ſmile of ſuch encouragement might nerve the
    fainteſt heart;
The crowd that follow'd after with good wiſhes
    cheer'd them on,
Some cried, " Stick to it, Thomas ; " others
    ſhouted, " Go it, John !"

VI.

Awake to competition, and alive to any game,
From Mancheſter and Liverpool the ſpeculators
    came ;
They calculated nicely every chance of loſs or
    gain ;
Some ſtak'd their caſh on cotton, ſome preferr'd
    the ſugar-cane.

VII.

Bold Thomas took precedence, as a proper man
    to lead,
And ſtraightway at a hedgerow cop he drove his
    gallant ſteed ;
He's off—he's on—he's over—is bold Thomas in
    his feat ?
Yes, the rider's in his ſaddle, and the horſe is on
    his feet !

H

VIII.

Make way for John ! the Leicefter Don ! John
    clear'd it far and wide,
And fcornfully he fmil'd on it when landed t'other
    fide ;
The prelude thus accomplifh'd without lofs of
    life or limb,
John's backers, much embolden'd, offer two to
    one on him.

IX.

Now John led off ; the choice again was fix'd
    upon a cop,
A rotten ditch in front of it, a rail upon the top;
While fhouts of " Bono Johnny!" to the echoing
    hills were fent,
He wink'd his eye, and at it, and right over it he
    went.

X.

Hold him lightly, Thomas, lightly, give him
    freedom ere he bound,
Why fhape your courfe with fo much force, to
    run yourfelf aground ?
Thus againft a Ruffian rampart goes a Britifh
    cannon ball :
Were Thomas at Sebaftopol, how fpeedily'twould
    fall

XI.

Would you gain that proud pre-eminence on
which your rival ſtands,
Upraiſe your voice, uprouſe your horſe, but ſlacken
both your hands;
'Tis vain, 'tis vain, his ſteed again ſtands planted
in the ditch,
The game is o'er, he tries no more, who makes a
ſecond hitch.

XII.

Thus, unlike the wars of Lancaſter and York,
in days of yore,
The Cheſter ſtrife with Leiceſter unexpeſtedly
was o'er;
We elſe had learnt which method beſt inſures us
from a fall,
The Cheſter on-and-off ſtep, or the Leiceſter,
clearing all?

XIII.

Whether breeches white, or breeches brown, the
more adheſive be,
And which the more effeſtive ſpur, Champagne
or Eau-de-vie?
Theſe, alas! and other problems which their pro-
greſs had reveal'd,
Remain unſettled queſtions for the future hunting
field.

XIV.

One leffon learn, young ladies all, who came to
    fee the fhow,
Remember, in the race of life, once only to fay
    " No ; "
This moral, for your warning, to my ditty I
    attach,
May ye ne'er by two refufals altogether lofe a
    match !
    1854.

Tarporley Hunt Song.

I.

THE Eagle won Jupiter's favour,
    The Sparrow to Venus was dear,
The Owl of Minerva, though graver,
    We want not its gravity here ;
The Swallow flies faft, but remember
    The Swallow with Summer is gone,
What bird is there left in November
    To rival the Tarporley Swan ?

II.

Though fcarlet in colour our clothing,
    Our collars though green in their hue,
The red cap of liberty loathing,
    Each man is at heart a True Blue ;

Through life 'tis our fworn refolution,
  To ftick to the pig-fkin and throne;
We are all for a good conftitution,
  Each man taking care of his own.

III.

Though the Sailor, who rides on the ocean,
  With cheers may encounter the foe;
Wind and fteam, what are they to horfe motion?
  Sea cheers, to a land Tally ho?
The canvas, the fcrew, and the paddle
  The fpeed of a thorough-bred lack,
When faft in the fox-hunting faddle,
  We gallop aftern of the pack.

IV.

Quæfitum, that ftandard of merit,
  Where each his true level may know,
Checks pride in the haughty of fpirit,
  Emboldens the timid and flow;
The liquor that fparkles before us,
  The dumb when they drink it can fpeak,
While the deaf in the roar of our chorus
  A cure for their malady feek.

V.

Forget not that other Red Jacket,
  Turn'd up with green laurel and bay!
The tri-colour'd banners that back it!
  The might of their mingled array!

Forget not the deeds that unite 'em
  As comrades, though rivals in fame;
But fill to the brim that quæſitum
  Which Friendſhip and Chivalry claim.
    1855.

A Remonſtrance on Lord Stanley's Suggeſtion
that the Seſſion of Parliament ſhould be
held during the Winter Months.

JOY! when November bids our ſport begin,
  When ringing echoes through the vale re-
    ſound,
When light of heart we to the ſaddle bound,
And health and pleaſure from the paſtime win.
Theſe muſt I barter for the Senate's din?
  Forego the muſic of the tuneful hound
  For midnight rant in adverſe clamour drown'd?
Lay by the whip to be myſelf whipp'd in?
Debaters! liſten, while the Chace propounds
  Her precepts—words too many work delay;
Your babblers draft, as we our tonguey hounds;
Rate without mercy thoſe who riot run;
  Let thoſe ſpeak only who have aught to ſay,
Speak to the point, and ſtop when they have
    done.
    1855.

Highwayfide.

A FAVOURITE FIXTURE DURING THE

CHESHIRE DIFFICULTY.

I.

RARE luck for the Chefhire, warn'd out
from the field,
That the Highway fuch endlefs diverfion can
yield ;
That the Huntfman can ftill with no covers to
draw,
Blow his horn on the road without breaking the
law.

II.

'Twixt highways and byeways ftill ringing the
change,
From gravel and fand to McAdam they range ;
When quite on the pavé their gallop reftrain,
And a jogtrot enjoy down a hard Chefhire lane.

III.

Steeds good in dirt, let the feather-weights urge
Slapdafh through the mud that encumbers the
verge,

Let heavy ones follow the track of the 'Bus,
Shouting, *Ibis in medio tutiffimus.*

IV.

They may jump on and off o'er the broken ftone
    heap,
In triangular fenders find timber to leap,
The towing path too may afford them a run
Juft to keep the game going and vary the fun.

V.

No alarm the moft timid old gentleman feels,
Babes may perambulate, hunting on wheels;
Dyfpepfy and gout the amufement may fhare,
So go it, ye cripples! and take a Bath chair.

VI.

The ufe of the mileftone, now coaching is done,
Is to meafure exactly the length of a run;
While each tap on the road they alternately try,
Till Tom fees two double with only one eye.

VII.

With fuch fport has this mud-larking lately
    fupplied 'em,
The Huntfman has call'd his crack horfe
    Rodum-Sidum,

Who dare fay thefe hounds have had nothing to do,
Highwayfide for their fixture the whole feafon
  through ?
1856.

Count Warnoff.

I.

WHEN the war with our Mufcovite foemen
  was o'er,
Then the *Offs* and the *Koffs* came to vifit our
  fhore ;
Their hard and ftern features your heart would
  appal,
But the face of Count Warnoff was fterneft of all;
  A terrible man was Count Warnoff !
    As cold as the fnow
    That envelopes Mofcow
  Was the heart of this horrid Count Warnoff !

II.

Woe ! woe ! to the fport of the fox-hunting
  Squire
When the Count fet his foot in this peaceable
  fhire !
So clean his own hands, his own morals fo ftrict,
A hole in each Redcoat he prefently pick'd ;

Such a virtuous man was Count Warnoff;
    Without fpeck of dirt
    You muft ride with clean fkirt
If the wrath you'd avert of Count Warnoff!

III.

The Count could not tolerate foible or folly,
He never made love, and he never got jolly;
He vow'd that fox-hunting he'd have at no price
Unlefs horfes and men were alike free from
        vice;
    Such a virtuous man was Count Warnoff!
        We muft all be good boys
        Or farewell to the joys
    Of the chace, if we nettle Count Warnoff!

IV.

Low whifper'd the huntfman (left mifchief befall
        him),
" I don't like the look of that Count What-d'ye-
        call him?"
Tom wink'd his blind eye as he lifted his cap,
" He's a rum 'un, fir, ain't he, that Mufcovy
        chap?"
    Such a terrible bugbear was Warnoff!
        Not a brufh, nor a pad
        In the fhire could be had,
    Such a terrible bugbear was Warnoff!

V.

He lock'd all the gates and he wir'd all the gaps,
And the woods were all planted with fpikes and
    fteel traps ;
No more the earth-ftoppers were dragg'd their
    warm beds off,
The nags in the ftable ftood eating their heads
    off ;
    Such a terrible man was Count Warnoff !
        Little children grew pale
        As their nurfe told the tale
    Of this terrible ogre, Count Warnoff !

VI.

Cheer up, my good fellows, Count Warnoff is
    gone !
Gone back to the banks of the Volga and Don ;
He may warn us, and welcome, from off his own
    fnow,
From the land where no fox-hunter wifhes to go ;
        But to bother our pack
        May he never come back
    To this peaceable county, Count Warnoff !

1857.

Le Gros-Veneur.

SUNG AT THE TARPORLEY HUNT MEETING,
NOVEMBER, 1858.

I.

A MIGHTY great hunter in deed and in name
To our fhire long ago with the Conqueror
came;
A hunting he went with his bugle and bow,
And he fhouted in Normandy-French " Tally-
Ho!"

*The man we now place at the head of our Chace
Can his pedigree trace from Le Gros-Veneur!*

II.

'Tis a maxim by fox-hunters well underftood,
That in horfes and hounds there is nothing like
blood;
So the chief who the fame of our kennel maintains
Should be born with the pureft of blood in his
veins!

*The man we now place at the head of our Chace
Can his pedigree trace from Le Gros-Veneur!*

III.

Old and young with delight fhall the Grof-
Veneur greet,
The field once again in good fellowfhip meet,

The fhire with one voice fhall re-echo our choice,
And again the old paftime all Chefhire rejoice !
> *May the fport we enfure many feafons endure,*
> *And the Chief of our Chace be Le Gros-Veneur!*

IV.

Though no more, as of yore, a long-bow at his
    back,
Now a Gros-Veneur guides us and governs our
    pack ;
Again let each earth-ftopper rife from his bed,
This year they fhall all be well fee'd and well fed.
> *May the fport we enfure many feafons endure,*
> *And the Chief of our Chace be Le Gros-Veneur!*

v.

Let Geoffrey with fmiles and with fhillings reftore
Good humour when houfewives their poultry
    deplore,
Well pleas'd, for each goofe on which Reynard
    has prey'd
To find in their pockets a golden egg laid !
> *May the fport we enfure many feafons endure,*
> *And the Chief of our Chace be Le Gros-Veneur!*

VI.

Should our Chief with the toil of the fenate grow
    pale,
The elixir of life is a ride o'er the vale ;

There, of health, fays the fong, he fhall gain a new
    ftock
" Till his pulfe beats the feconds as true as a
    clock."
May the fport we enfure many feafons endure,
And the Chief of our Chace be Le Gros-Veneur!

VII.

I defy Norman-dy now to fend a Chaffeur
Who can ride alongfide of our own Gros-Veneur!
And, couching my lance, I will challenge all
    France
To outvie the bright eye of the LADY CONSTANCE!
    Long, long, may fhe grace with her prefence
        our Chace,
    The Bride and the Pride of Le Gros-Veneur!

The Keeper.

I.

RUFUS KNOX, his lordfhip's keeper, is a
    formidable chap,
So at leaft think all who liften to his fwagger at
    the tap;
Ain't he up to poachers? ain't he down upon 'em
    too?
This very night he'd face and fight a dozen of
    the crew.

II.

With the Squire who hunts the country he is ever
 in difgrace,
For " Vulpicide " is written in red letters on his
 face ;
His oath that in one cover he a brace of foxes
 faw,
Is the never-failing prelude. that foretokens a
 blank draw.

III.

The moufing owl he fpares not, flitting through
 the twilight dim,
The beak it wears, it is, he fwears, too hook'd a
 one for him ;
In every woodland fongfter he fufpects a fecret
 foe,
His ear no mufic toucheth, fave the roofting
 pheafant's crow.

IV.

His ftoppers and his beaters, for the battue day
 array'd,
Behold him in his glory at the head of the brigade ;
That day on which a twelvemonth's toil trium-
 phantly is crown'd,
That day to him the pivot upon which the year
 turns round.

V.

There is a fpot where birds are fhot by fifties as
    they fly,
If envious of that ftation you muft tip him on the
    fly;
Confpicuous on the flaughter card if foremoft you
    would be,
That place like other places muft be purchas'd
    with a fee.

A Railway Accident with the Chefhire.

FEBRUARY 5TH, 1859.

I.

BY the fide of Poole cover laft Saturday ftood
    A hundred good horfes, both cocktail and
    blood;
Nor long ftood they idle, three deep in array,
Ere Reynard by Edwards was hollo'd away.

II.

Away! over meadow, away! over plough,
Away! down the dingle, away! up the brow!
"If you like not that fence, fir, get out of the
    way,
If one minute you lofe you may lofe the whole
    day."

III.

Away! through the evergreens,—laurel and box,
They may fcreen a cock-robin but not a run fox ;
As he pafs'd the henrooft at the Rookery Hall,
"Excufe me," faid pug, "I have no time to call."

IV.

The rail to our left and the river in front
Into two rival parties now fever'd the hunt ;
I will tell by-and-by which were right and which
  wrong,
Meanwhile let us follow the fox with our fong.

V.

Away! to the Weaver, whofe banks are foft fand,
" Look out, boys, ahead, there's a horfe-bridge
  at hand."
One by one the frail plank we crofs'd cautioufly
  o'er,
I had time juft to count that we number'd a fcore.

VI.

Though faft fox and hounds, there were men, by
  my troth,
Whofe ambition it was to go fafter than both ;
If that grey in the fkurry efcap'd a difafter,
Little thanks the good animal ow'd to its mafter.

I

VII.

Now Hornby went crafhing through bullfinch
    and rail
With Brancker befide him on Murray's rat tail;
Two green collars only were feen in this flight,
Squire Warburton one, and the other John
    White.

VIII.

Where was Maffey, who found us the fox that
    we run?
Where Philip the father? where Philip the fon?
Where was Grofvenor our Guide? where was
    bold Shrewfberie?
We had with us one *Earle,* how I wifh we'd
    had three!

IX.

Where Talbot? where Lyon? though failing away
They were both fadly out of their bearings that
    day;
Where Lafcelles, De Trafford, Brooke, Corbet
    and Court?
They muft take return tickets if bent upon fport.

X.

Sailors, railers and tailors! what can you now do?
If you hope to nick in, the next ftation is Crewe;

Second-clafs well difpers'd, it was only clafs firft
Which, efcaping the boiler, came in for the burft!

XI.

Away! with red rowel, away! with flack rein
For twenty-five minutes to Wiftafton Lane,
Where a check gave relief both to rider and horfe,
Where again the fplit field re-united its force.

XII.

From that point we turn'd back and continued
　　our chace
To the gorfe where we found, but more fober
　　the pace ;
Reynard, fkirting Poole Hall, trying fand-earth
　　and drain,
Was at length by the pack, who deferv'd him,
　　o'erta'en.

XIII.

While they worry their fox a fhort word I would
　　fay,
Of advice to thofe riders who rode the wrong
　　way,
Who were forc'd to put up with fkim-milk for
　　their fun,
For the fkurry had fkimm'd off the cream of the
　　run :

XIV.

" As a coverfide hack you may prudently ftick
" To the line of the rail, it is eafy and quick;
" But when fox and faft hounds on a fkurry are
        bent,
" The line you fhould ftick to is that of the fcent."

Tarporley Hunt Song.

1859.

I.

NAMES, honour'd of old, on our Club-book
        enroll'd,
It were fhame fhould their fucceffors flight 'em,
They who Horace could quote, and who firft of
        all wrote
On our Tarporley glaffes " Quæfitum ;"
        O, famous Quæfitum !
        Famous in ftory Quæfitum !
There has pafs'd very nigh a full century by
Since our fathers firft fill'd a Quæfitum.

II.

Old Bacchus fo jolly, who hates melancholy,
Our founders, how can he requite 'em ?
From the land of the vine let the beft of his wine
Be referv'd to o'erflow the Quæfitum ;

O, famous Quæſitum !
Jolly Bacchus, fill up the Quæſitum !
Whether claret or port, it muſt be the beſt ſort,
If it fit be to fill a Quæſitum.

III.

The goblet, methinks, from which Jupiter drinks,
With thunder-cheer *ter repetitum*,
Since when Juno was gone he turn'd into the
    Swan,
Should be chang'd for a cryſtal Quæſitum ;
    O, famous Quæſitum !
    Fit for Olympus, Quæſitum !
Cup-bearer Hebe, how happy would ſhe be
With neƈtar to fill a Quæſitum.

IV.

Thoſe who dar'd with rude eye at Diana to ſpy,
She unkennel'd her pack to affright 'em ;
She who ſmiles with delight on our banquet to-
    night,
Bids us fill to the chace a Quæſitum ;
    Fill, fill the Quæſitum !
    To the heart-ſtirring chace a Quæ-
    ſitum ;
She who ſheds her bright beam upon fountain and
    ſtream
With her ſmile ſhall make bright the Quæſitum.

V.

One bumper ftill let all fox-hunters fill,
'Tis a toaft that will fondly excite 'em,
Since the brave can alone claim the fair as their
    own,
Let us drink to our loves a Quæfitum ;
      Fill, fill the Quæfitum !
        A glowing o'erflowing Quæfitum !
From Beauty's fweet lip he who kiffes would
    fip,
With his own muft firft kifs the Quæfitum.

VI.

Again ere I end, all who foxes befriend,
Let a bumper thrice honour'd delight 'em,
May the forward and faft ftill be up at the laft,
Give the flow ones another Quæfitum ;
      Fill, fill the Quæfitum !
        To good fellows all a Quæfitum !
Let him faft be or flow, each fhall prove ere we
    go,
An excufe for another Quæfitum.

A " Burſt " in the Ball Week.

JANUARY 19, 1860.

I.

WE had danc'd the night through,
Till the candles burnt blue,
But were all in the ſaddle next morn ;
Once again with Tom Rance,
In broad daylight to dance
To the muſic of hollo and horn.

II.

We were all giddy ſtill
With the waltz and quadrille,
When arous'd by the loud " Tallyho !"
I muſt tune my faſt rhyme
Up to double-quick time,
For the movement was *preſtiſſimo.*

III.

The fox by one hound
Near the Smoker was found—
As he wip'd that dog's noſe with his bruſh,
" I don't mean to die,"
Said bold Reynard, " not I ;
Nor care I for Edwards one ruſh."

IV.

With a fox of fuch pluck,
'Twas a piece of rare luck
    That no ploughboy to turn him was near;
That no farmer was there
At the gem'men to fwear,
    No tailor to head his career.

V.

Some, to lead off the ball,
Get away firft of all,
    Some linger too long at *pouffette*;
Down the middle fome go,
In the deep ditch below,
    Thrown out ere they *up again* get.

VI.

One, pitch'd from his feat,
Was compell'd, with wet feet,
    His heels in the gutter to cool;
While his horfe, in full fwing,
Danc'd a new Highland fling,
    He himfelf ftood and danc'd a *pas feul.*

VII.

" Tell me, Edwards," faid one,
When the fkurry was done,
    " How long were we running this rig?"

" To keep time, indeed, fir,
I little take heed, fir,
　When dancing the Tallyho jig."

VIII.

But the time I can tell,
And the fpot I know well,
　Where the huntfman his fox overtook;
Twenty-five minutes good,
When he reach'd Arley Wood,
　Where he died on the banks of the brook.

IX.

I could name the few firft
Who went beft in this burft;
　I could tell how the fteady ones rac'd;
But fince all were content
With the pace themfelves went,
　What matters it where they were plac'd?

X.

If a live fox fhould run,
As that dead one has done,
　O'er this country again, by good chance,
May I have my fleet bay
For a partner that day,
　And be juft where I was in the dance.

Farmer Newſtyle and Farmer Oldſtyle.

I.

"GOOD day," ſaid Farmer Oldſtyle, taking
  Newſtyle by the arm ;
"I be cum to look aboit me, wilt 'ee ſhow me o'er
  thy farm ?"
Young Newſtyle took his wideawake, and lighted
  a cigar,
And ſaid, "Won't I aſtoniſh you, old-faſhioned
  as you are !

II.

"No doubt you have an aneroid? ere ſtarting,
  you ſhall ſee
How truly mine prognoſticates what weather
  there will be."
"I aint got no ſuch gimcrack, but I knows
  there'll be a fluſh
When I ſees th' oud ram tak' ſhelter wi' his tail
  agen a buſh."

III.

"Allow me, firſt, to ſhow you the analyſis I
  keep,
And the compounds to explain of this experi-
  mental heap,

Where hydrogen, and nitrogen, and oxygen
abound,
To haften germination and to fertilize the
ground."

IV.

" A pratty foight o' larning you have pil'd up of
a ruck ;
The only name it went by in my feyther's time
was muck ;
I knows not how that tool you calls a *nollyfis* may
work ;
I turns it, when it's rotten, pretty handy wi' a
fork."

V.

" A famous pen of Cotfwolds ! Pafs your hand
along the back—
Fleeces fit for ftuffing the Lord Chancellor's
woolfack !
For premiums e'en Inquifitor would own thefe
wethers *are* fit ;
If you want to purchafe good 'uns you muft go
to Mr. Garfit.

VI.

" Two bulls firft-rate, of different breeds—the
judges all proteft
Both are fo fuper-excellent, they know not which
is beft ;

Fair, could he fee this Ayrſhire, would with jea-
   louſy be ril'd,
That hairy one's a Welſhman, and was bred by
   Mr. Wild."

VII.

" Well, well, that little hairy bull he ſhanna be
   ſo bad ;
But what be yonder beaſt I hear a bellowing like
   mad,
A ſnortin fire and ſmoke out?—be it ſome big
   Rooſian gun ?
Or be it twenty bullocks ſquz together into one ?"

VIII.

" My ſteam Faɛtotum that, ſir, doing all I have
   to do—
My ploughman, and my reaper, and my jolly
   thraſher, too ;
Steam's yet but in its infancy, no mortal man
   alive
Can tell to what perfeɛtion modern farming will
   arrive."

IX.

" Steam, as yet, is but an infant "———He had
   ſcarcely ſaid the word
When through the tottering farmſtead was a loud
   exploſion heard ;

The engine dealing death around, deſtruction and
    diſmay ;
Though ſteam be but an infant, this indeed
    was no child's play.

x.

The women ſcream'd like blazes as the blazing
    hayrick burn'd,
The ſucking pigs were in a crack all into crack-
    ling turn'd ;
Grill'd chickens clog the hen-coop, roaſted duck-
    lings choke the gutter,
And turkeys round the poultry-yard on devil'd
    pinions flutter.

xi.

Two feet deep in buttermilk the ſtoker's two
    feet lie,
The cook, before ſhe bakes it, finds a finger in
    the pie ;
The labourers for their loſt legs were looking
    round the farm,
They could not lend a hand becauſe they had
    not got an arm.

xii.

Oldſtyle, all ſoot from head to foot, look'd like a
    big black ſheep ;
Newſtyle was thrown upon his own experi-
    mental heap :

" That weather-glafs," faid Oldftyle, " canna
    be in proper fettle,
Or it might as well a tou'd us there was thunder
    in the kettle."

XIII.

" Steam is fo expanfive." " Ay," faid Old-
    ftyle, " fo I fee ;
So expenfive, as you call it, that it wunna do for
    me ;
According to my notion, that's a beaft that canna
    pay,
Who champs up for his morning feed a hundred
    ton o' hay."

XIV.

Then to himfelf, faid Oldftyle, as he homewards
    quickly went,
" I'll tak' no farm where th' doctor's bill be
    heavier than the rent ;
I've never in hot water been ; fteam fhanna
    fpeed *my* plough,
I would liefer thrafh my oats out by the fweat of
    my own brow.

XV.

" I neether want to fcald my pigs, nor toaft my
    cheefe, not I,
Afore the butcher fticks 'em, or the factor comes
    to buy ;

They fhanna catch me here again to rifk my
    limbs and loif ;
I've nought at whoam to blow me up, except it
    be my woif."

Home with the Hounds ; or, the

Huntfman's Lament.

I.

OVER-RIDDEN ! over-ridden !
    All along of that the check ;
When the ditch that gemman flid in,
    Don't I wifh he'd broke his neck.
I to hunt my hounds am able,
    Would the field but play me fair ;
Mobb'd at Smithfield by the rabble,
    Who a fox could follow there ?

II.

Let the tinker ride his kettle,
    Let the tailor ride his goofe,
How can hounds to hunting fettle
    With the like o' them let loofe ?
What's the ufe on't when he fcrambles
    Through a run that butchers tit ?
Butcher'd foxhounds for the fhambles
    They be neither fat nor fit.

III.

What's the ufe o' jockies thumping
    Wi' their 'andwhips bits of blood ?
Tits by inftinct fhy of jumping,
    For they could not if they would ;
Though the fnob, who cannot guide her,
    Mounts the mare as draws his trap ;
'Taint the red coat makes the rider,
    Leathers, boots, nor yet the cap.

IV.

They who come their coats to fhow, they
    Better were at home in bed ;
What of hounds and hunting know they ?
    Nothing elfe but " go ahead ; "
At the Kennel I could train 'em,
    If they would but come to fchool,
Two and two in couples chain 'em,
    Feed on meal, and keep 'em cool.

V.

Gemmen, gemmen, fhame upon 'em,
    Plague my heart out worfe than all,
Worfe than Bowdon mobs at Dunham,
    Worfe than cobblers at Poole Hall ;
Spurring at a fence their clippers,
    When the hounds are in the rear !
Reg'lar gemmen ! felf and whippers
    Tipping reg'lar once a year !

VI.

Well! foft folder next I'll try on,
  Rating only riles a fwell;
Mifter Brancker! Mifter Lyon!
  Mifter Hornby!—hope you're well;
'Taint the pack that I'm afraid on,
  And I likes to fee you firft,
But when fo much fteam be laid on
  Beant you fear'd the copper'll burft?

VII.

Rantipole, I fee'd him fprawling
  Underneath a horfe's hoof;
Prudence only heerd me calling
  Juft in time to keep aloof;
Vulcan lam'd for life! Old *Victor*
  Ne'er again will he fhow fight;
Venus, fin that gelding kick'd her,
  Aint he fpoilt her beauty quite?

VIII.

Gentlemen, unto my thinking,
  Should behave themfelves as fich;
'Tik'lar when the fcent is finking,
  And the hounds are at a hitch;
How my temper can I mafter,
  Fretted till I fume and foam?
I can only backwards caft, or
  Blow my horn and take 'em home.

K

On hearing that "The Chefhire" were to hunt Five Days a Week.

"THERE'S luck in odd numbers," fays Rory
O'More,
" Five days," fays fquire Corbet, "good fport
will enfure;"
So, *All-fours* out of fafhion, the game is now *Fives*,
But who cares what they call it while Fox-hunting
thrives ?

We are all of us Tailors in Turn.

I.

I WILL fing you a fong of a fox-hunting bout,
They fhall tell their own tale who to-day
were thrown out;
For the fafteft as well as the floweft of men,
Snobs or top-fawyers, alike now and then,
                We are all of us tailors in turn.

II.

Says one, " From the cover I ne'er got away,
Old Quidnunc fat quoting *The Times* on his Grey,
How Lord Derby was wrong, and Lord Aber-
deen right,
And the hounds, ere he finifh'd were clean out
of fight."
                We are all of us tailors in turn.

III.

Says one, "When we ftarted o'er fallow and
    grafs,
I was clofe at the tail of the hounds, but, alas !
We came down to a drain in that black-bottom'd
    fen,
O had I but been on my brook-jumper, then ! "—
        We are all of us tailors in turn.

IV.

" Difmounting," fays one, " at a gate that was
    faft,
The crowd, pufhing through, knock'd me down
    as it pafs'd ;
My horfe feized the moment to take his own fling,
Who'll again do, out hunting, a good-natured
    thing ! "
        We are all of us tailors in turn.

V.

" Down the lane went I merrily failing along,
Till I found," fays another, " my courfe was all
    wrong ;
I thought that his line toward the breeding-earth
    lay,
But he went, I've heard fince, juft the oppofite
    way."
        We are all of us tailors in turn.

VI.

From the wine-cup o'er night fome were forry
        and fick,
Some fkirted, fome cran'd, and fome rode for a
        nick ;
Like whales, in the water, fome flounder'd about,
Thrown off and thrown in, they were alfo thrown
        out.
        We are all of us tailors in turn.

VII.

" You will find in the field a whole ton of loft
        fhoes."—
A credulous blackfmith, believing the news,
Thought his fortune were made if he walk'd
        o'er the ground ;—
He loft a day's work, but he ne'er a fhoe found !
        We are all of us tailors in turn.

VIII.

What deeds would one hero have done on his
        Grey,
Who was nowhere at all on his Cheftnut to-day !
All join in the laugh when a braggart is beat,
And that jeft is lov'd beft which is aim'd at conceit.
        We are all of us tailors in turn.

IX.

Good fellows there are, unpretending and flow,
Who can ne'er be thrown out, for they ne'er
    mean to go ;
But, when the run's over, thefe oftentimes tell
The ftory far better than they who went well.
          We are all of us tailors in turn.

X.

How trifling a caufe will oft lofe us a run !
From the find to the finifh how few fee the fun !
A mifchance, it is call'd, when we come to a
    halt ;
I ne'er heard of one who confefs'd it a fault,
          Yet we're all of us tailors in turn.

A Word ere we Start.

I.

BOYS, to the hunting field ! though 'tis No-
    vember,
  The wind's in the fouth ;—but a word ere we
    ftart.—
Though keenly excited, I bid you remember
  That hunting's a fcience, and riding an art.

II.

The order of march and the due regulation
  That guide us in warfare, we need in the
    chace—
Huntfman and Whip, each his own proper ftation,
  Horfe, hound and fox, each his own proper
    place.

III.

The fox takes precedence of all from the cover;
  The horfe is an animal purpofely bred
After the pack to be ridden, not *over*—
  Good hounds are not rear'd to be knock'd on
    the head.

IV.

Strong be your tackle, and carefully fitted,
  Breaft-plate and bridle, girth, ftirrup, and chain;
You will need not two arms, if the mouth be well
    bitted,
  One hand lightly us'd will fuffice for the rein.

V.

Buckfkin's the only wear fit for the faddle;
  Hats for Hyde Park, but a cap for the chace;
In tops of black leather let fifhermen paddle,
  The calves of a fox-hunter white ones incafe.

VI.

If your horfe be well bred and in blooming con-
dition,
Both up to the country and up to your weight,
O, then give the reins to your youthful ambition,
Sit down in your faddle and keep his head
ftraight!

VII.

Paftime for princes!—prime fport of our nation!
Strength in their finew and bloom on their
cheek;
Health to the old, to the young recreation;
All for enjoyment the hunting-field feek.

VIII.

Eager and emulous only, not fpiteful;—
Grudging no friend, though ourfelves he may
beat;
Juft enough danger to make fport delightful!
Toil juft fufficient to make flumber fweet!

Hard-riding Dick.

I.

FROM the cradle his name has been " Hard-
riding Dick,"
Since the time when cock-horfe he beftraddled
a ftick;

Since the time when, unbreech'd, without faddle
    or rein,
He kick'd the old donkey along the green lane.

II.

Dick, wafting no time o'er the claffical page,
Spent his youth in the ftable without any wage ;
The life of poor Dick, when he enter'd his teens,
Was to fleep in the hay-loft and breakfaft on beans.

III.

Promoted'at length, Dick's adventures began:—
A ftripling on foot, but when mounted a man ;
Capp'd, booted, and fpurr'd, his young foul was
    on fire,
The day he was dubb'd " Second Whip " to the
    Squire.

IV.

See, how Dick, like a dart, fhoots a-head of the
    pack !
How he ftops, turns, and twifts, rates, and rattles
    them back !
The laggard exciting, controlling the rafh,
He can comb down a hair with the point of his
    lafh.

V.

O ! fhow me that country which Dick cannot
    crofs—
Be it open or wood, be it upland or mofs,

Through the fog or the funfhine, the calm or the
  fquall,
By day-light or ftar-light, or no light at all !

VI.

Like a fwallow can Dick o'er the water-flood fkim,
And Dick, like a duck, in the faddle can fwim ;
Up the fteep mountain-fide like a cat he can crawl,
He can fqueeze like a moufe through a hole in
  the wall !

VII.

He can tame the wild young one, infpirit the old,
The reftive, the runaway, handle and hold ;
Sharp fteel or foft-folder, which e'er does the trick,
It makes little matter to Hard-riding Dick.

VIII.

Bid the chief from the Defert bring hither his
  mare,
To ride o'er the plain againft Dick if he dare ;
Bring Coffack or Mexican, Spaniard or Gaul,
There's a Dick in our village will ride round them
  all !

IX.

A whip is Dick's fceptre, a faddle Dick's throne,
And a horfe is the kingdom he rules as his own ;
While grafping ambition encircles the earth,
The dominions of Dick are enclofed in a girth.

X.

Three ribs hath he broken, two legs, and one arm,
But there hangs, it is faid, round his neck a life-
    charm;
Still long odds are offer'd that Dick, when he drops,
Will die, as he lived, in his breeches and tops.

Thompſon's Trip to Epſom.

I.

KIND friends! delighted Thompſon! on the
    night he came to town
They faid: "If up to Epſom, we will call and
    take you down."
Next morn, ere Boots awoke him, there was feen
    at Thompſon's door
The coach the ladies fat in and the fatin that they
    wore.

II.

Poor Thompſon's had no breakfaſt! how could he
    his bacon fave,
How cut his mutton-chops up when his own he
    could not fhave?
Poor Thompſon's had no breakfaſt! "Waiter,
    fay we cannot wait;"
With friends fo faſt his fate it was to faſt upon a
    fête!

III.

" We're full infide, for empties there's an empty
   dicky free,"
Alas ! ere long with Thompfon's heart all dicky
   will it be ;
Her beaming eye who tied his veil pierc'd thro'
   him like a lance,
Of what avail was fuch a veil to fhield from fuch
   a glance ?

IV.

Forgetting foon his breakfaft fpoon he takes a
   fpoony turn,
His heart feels hot within him like a heater in
   the urn ;
A fudden flip 'twixt cup and lip to Beauty from
   Bohea,
His tea no more he miffes, thinks no more of
   Mrs. T.

V.

A lottery they needs muft have upon the Derby
   day,
Fair fingers cut the tickets, fo of courfe it was fair
   play ;
My Lord, who draws the favourite, o'erwhelms
   them with his thanks,
Poor Thompfon's had no breakfaft ! fo they hand
   him all the blanks.

VI.

Poor Thompſon's had no breakfaſt ! it was whiſ-
  per'd in a tone
Which meant, if words a meaning have, " How
  hungry we are grown ! "
Poor Thompſon ſigh'd as they untied the hamper,
  Thompſon's ſigh,
Say was it for his ladie-love or for the pigeon pie ?

VII.

Poor Thompſon's had no breakfaſt ! looking
  down he now ſurveys
The fair inſiders filling their inſide with mayon-
  naiſe ;
For the luncheon ſtakes diſqualified was Thompſon, they declare,
A ſtomach twice as empty as their own would
  not be fair.

VIII.

Poor Thompſon's had no breakfaſt ! " Super-
  excellent this ham."
Poor Thompſon's had no breakfaſt ! " What a
  tender bit of lamb."
Poor Thompſon's had no breakfaſt ! " I prefer
  the dry champagne."
Poor Thompſon's had no breakfaſt ! " May I
  trouble you again ?"

IX.

When done at laſt their own repaſt poor Thompſon, better late
Than never, got poſſeſſion of the hamper and a
plate,
With two rejected drumſticks on a hollow diſh
he drums,
And chirps are heard as dicky-bird picks up the
scatter'd crumbs.

X.

Once more at home ſee Thompſon, in his breakfaſt parlour chair,
He knew better than to quarrel with his bread
and butter there;
His wife with indignation of his aching ſtomach
heard,
Of the heartache which had troubled him he
never ſaid a word.

A Modern Stable.

I.

BEHOLD the new ſtable his lordſhip has
built,
Its walls and its ſtalls painted, varniſh'd and
gilt;

No prince in his palace, King, Sultan, or Czar,
Was e'er lodg'd in fuch ftate as thefe quadrupeds
    are.

II.

Pitchfork and bucket, chain, buckle and rack,
Burnifh'd up till they fhine like the coats on their
    back ;
I fcarce know on which moft applaufe to beftow,
On the gildings above or the geldings below.

III.

What I marvell'd at moft, in the front of each
    ftall
Why a flab of blue flate fhould be fix'd in the
    wall ?
Why a horfe (and the query ftill puzzles my
    pate)
Like a fchoolboy fhould ftand with his eyes on a
    flate ?

IV.

Muft the heads of our horfes be cramm'd now a-
    day
With learning as well as their bellies with hay ?
Muft our yearlings be coach'd till their little go
    won,
The trainer has taught them " to read as they
    run."

On Reading in the " Times," April 9th,
1860, a Critique on the Life
of Aſheton Smith.

THE mighty Hunter taken to his reſt,
His cheriſh'd ſport now points the critic's
jeſt,
Pleas'd of a ſect facetiouſly to tell
A " meet" their heaven and a froſt their hell,
Who blindly follow, clad in coats of pink,
A beaſt whoſe nature is to run and ſtink;
When view'd, with ſhouts of frantic joy they
greet him,
Forbearing ſtill, when they have kill'd, to eat him,
His head enſhrin'd within a cryſtal caſe,
His " bruſh," a relic, on their walls they place.
In mad devotion to this beaſt unclean,
Encountering " Bullfinches" (whate'er that
mean)
They ride to fall and riſe again forthwith,
A ſect whoſe great high-prieſt was Aſheton
Smith.

Let him who laughs our noble ſport to ſcorn,
Meet me next year at Melton or at Quorn;

Let the faſt train by which his bolts are ſped
Bring down the Thunderer himſelf inſtead,
My cover hack (not Stamford owns a finer)
Can canter glibly like a penny-a-liner;
Free of my ſtable let him take the pick,
Not one when mounted but can do the trick;
Faſt as his pen can run, if he can ride,
The foremoſt few will find him at their ſide;
His leader left unfiniſh'd on the ſhelf,
To prove a leading article himſelf!

With cloſing daylight, when our paſtime ends,
Together dining, we will part good friends;
And home returning to his gas-lit court,
His mind enlighten'd by a good day's ſport,
Of hounds and hunting ſome ſlight knowledge
        then
Shall guide the gooſe-quill, when he writes again.

Tarporley Swan-Hopping.

NOVEMBER 6TH, 1862.

I.

WHEN a Swan takes to ſinging they ſay ſhe
        will die,
But our Tarporley Swan proves that legend a lie;

For a hundred years paft fhe has fwung at this door,
May fhe fwing there and fing there a thoufand
    years more !

II.

Rara avis in terris our Swan though not black,
Though white her own pinions and white her
    own back,
Still her flock, in November full-feather'd, are feen
Refplendent in plumage of fcarlet and green.

III.

Heralds fay fhe is fprung from that White Swan
    of yore
Which our Sires at Blore Heath to the battle-
    field bore ;
When, *Quæfitum meritis*, loyal and true,
Their fwords Chefhire men for Queen Margaret
    drew.

IV.

To and fro in her flight fhe has travers'd the Vale,
She has lov'd on an ocean of claret to fail ;
Whate'er takes her fancy fhe thinks it no fin,
So her dancing-days, now fhe's a hundred, begin.

V.

You have heard in your youth of the Butterfly's
    Ball,
How the birds and the beafts fhe invited them all ;

L

So the Tarporley Swan, not a whit lefs gallant,
Invites all her friends to a Soirée danfante.

VI.

Left her flock at the Ball fhould themfelves mif-
   behave,
The old Swan thus a lecture on etiquette gave:
" Though, my fons, o'er the Vale you make light
   of a fall,
Beware how you make a falfe ftep at the Ball.

VII.

" You muft all in good feather be dreft for the
   night,
Let not the Swan neck-tie be tied over-tight ;
Each his partner may fan with the tip of his wing,
Patent pumps for web feet will be quite the right
   thing.

VIII.

" Expand not your pinions, 'twere folly to try,
In vain would their vaftnefs with crinoline vie ;
Let no rude neck outftretch'd o'er the table be
   feen,
Nor ftand dabbling your bills in the fupper tureen.

IX.

" When you fail down the middle, or fwim through
   a dance,

With grace and with ftatelinefs, Swan-like, ad-
    vance,
Let your entrance, your exit no waddle difclofe,
But hold all your heads up, and turn out your toes.

X.

" To the counfel convey'd in thefe motherly
    words
Give heed, and I truft you will all be good birds ;
I give you my blefling and bid you begone,
So away to the Ball with you, every one."

Killing no Murder.

I KNOW not—fearch all England round,
    If better Huntfman can be found,
A bolder rider or a neater,
When mounted for the field, than Peter ;
But this I know, there is not one
So bent on blood as Collifon.
Hear now the doctrine he propounds,
All ye who love to follow hounds :—

Says he, " Since firft my horn was blown,
This maxim have I made my own ;
Kill if you can with fport ;—but ftill—
Or with it or without it,—kill.

A feather in my cap to pin,
A frefh one every brufh I win !
That fox is doom'd who feeks for reft
In gorfe or fpinney when diftreft ;
Though far and faft he may have fped,
He counts for nothing till he's dead.
I hold that Whip not worth his pay,
Who fails to keep him there at bay ;
When round and round the coverfide
The mounted mob, like madmen, ride,
Now crofs him here, now head him there,
While fhouts and clamour rend the air.
Spare him, the gentle folk may fay,
To live and fight another day ;
Upon my coat confpicuous feen,
All know me by my collar green,
I fhould myfelf be greener ftill,
Were I to fpare when I could kill ;
Excufe me, gentlemen, I fay
My hounds have had but two to-day.

" When April ends the hunting year,
How then fhould I in *Bell* appear ?
Or how my brother Huntfmen face
If fhort of booking fifty brace ?
There's nothing, I maintain, abfurder
Than to fay that killing's Murder."
        1865.

On Peter Collison's late Fall.

1868.

BAD luck betide that treacherous fpot
 Where Peter's horfe, though at a trot,
Roll'd over, hurling headlong there
A Huntfman whom we ill could fpare ;
As there he lay and gafp'd for breath,
Unconfcious quite and pale as death,
The clinging hounds around him yell,
And wailing moans their forrow tell.
Let ——, who over-rides them all,
Take warning by our Huntfman's fall ;
When fuch fhall be that rider's fate
(And his it will be foon or late),
They o'er the downfal of their foe
Will not upraife the voice of woe ;
When proftrate, if the pack fhould greet him
With open mouths, 'twill be to eat him.

Riding to Hounds.

No inconfiderate rafhnefs, or vain appetite
Of falfe encountering formidable things ;
But a true fcience of diftinguifhing
  *   *   *   *   *

BEN JONSON.

A S when two dogs in furious combat clofe,
   The bone forgotten whence the ftrife arofe,
Some village cur fecures the prize unfeen,
And, while the maftiffs battle, picks it clean ;
So when two horfemen, joftling fide by fide,
Heed not the pack, but at each other ride,
More glorious ftill the loftier fences deem,
And face the brook where wideft flows the ftream;
One breathlefs fteed, when fpurs no more avail,
Rolls o'er the cop, and hitches on the rail ;
One floundering lies—to watery ditch confign'd,
While laughing fchool-boy leaves them both
     behind,
Pricks on his pony 'till the brufh be won,
And bears away the honours of the run.

Newby Ferry.

I.

T HE morning was mild as a morning in
   May,
Slingfby on Saltfifh was out for the day ;

Though the Ure was rain-fwollen, the pack,
    dafhing in,
Follow'd clofe on the fox they had found at the
    Whin.

II.

They have crofs'd it full cry, but the horfemen
    are ftay'd,
The ford is too deep for the boldeft to wade ;
So to Newby they fped, like an army difpers'd,
Hoping each in his heart to be there with the firft.

III.

Lloyd, Robinfon, Orvis, and Slingfby the brave,
Preffing on to that ferry to find there a grave ;
Little thought the four comrades when, rivals in
    pace,
With fuch hafte they fpurr'd on that they rode a
    death-race.

IV.

Orvis now cries, in a voice of defpair,
"They're away far ahead, and not one of us there !
Quickly, good ferrymen, haul to the fhore,
Bad luck to your craft if we catch 'em no more ! "

V.

Thus fhouting, old Orvis leapt down to the bank,

And with Lloyd alongſide led his horſe to the
    plank;
There ſtood they, diſmounted, their hands on the
    rein,
Never more to ſet foot in the ſtirrup again!

VI.

Eleven good men in the laden boat,
Eleven good ſteeds o'er the ferry float;
Alas! ere their ferrymen's taſk was done,
Two widows were weeping o'er father and ſon!

VII.

What meaneth that ſudden and piercing cry
From the horſemen who ſtood on the bank hard by?
The ſhadow of death ſeem'd to darken the wave,
And the torrent to pauſe as it open'd a grave.

VIII.

Slingſby is ſinking—his ſtretch'd arm had clung
To the rein of his horſe as he overboard ſprung;
The barque, overburden'd, bends down on her ſide,
Heels o'er, and her freight is engulf'd in the tide.

IX.

In that moment an age ſeem'd to intervene
Ere Vyner was firſt on the ſurface ſeen;

The plank fcarcely won ere his arm he extends
To reach and to refcue his finking friends.

X.

Whips knotted faft, in the hafte of defpair,
Reach not the doom'd who were drowning there ;
Swimmers undauntedly breafted the wave,
Till themfelves were nigh funk in their efforts to
    fave.

XI.

Robinfon (he who could bird-like fkim
O'er fence and o'er fallow) unpraĉtis'd to fwim,
Hopelefs of aid in this uttermoft need,
Save in the ftrength of his gallant fteed !

XII.

Slowly that horfe from the river's bed,
Still back'd by his rider, uprais'd his head ;
But the noftrils' faint breath and the terror-glaz'd
    eye
Tell how vain is all hope with its fury to vie.

XIII.

Unappall'd, who could gaze on the heart-rending
    fight ?
His rider unmov'd, in the faddle upright,

Calm for one moment, and then the death fcream
As down, ftill unfeated, he fank in the ftream !

XIV.

Slingfby meanwhile from the waters uprofe,
Where deepeft and ftrongeft the mid-current
   flows ;
Manfully ftemming its onward courfe,
He ftruck for the boat with his failing force.

XV.

Then feebly one arm was uplifted, in vain
Striving to fnatch at the cheftnut's mane;
For that faithful fteed, through the rolling tide,
Had fwum like a dog to his mafter's fide.

XVI.

At length by the ftream he can buffet no more,
Borne, bleeding and pale, to the farther fhore,
There, as the Slingfbys had ofttimes lain,
Lay the laft of that Houfe in his harnefs flain !

XVII.

Sprung from a knightly and time-honour'd race,
Pride of thy county, and chief of her chace !
Though a ftranger, not lefs is his forrow fincere,

Who now weeps o'er the clofe of thy gallant
career.

XVIII.

Let Yorkſhire, while England re-echoes her wail,
Bereft of her braveſt, record the ſad tale,
How Slingſby of Scriven at Newby fell,
In the heat of that chace which he lov'd ſo well.

Hunting Song.

I.

OF all the recreations with which mortal man
    is bleſt,
Go where he will, fox-hunting ſtill is pleaſanteſt
    and beſt ;
The hunter knows no ſorrow here, the cup of
    life to him,
A bumper bright of freſh delight fill'd ſparkling
    to the brim.
Away, away we go,
With a tally, tally ho,
With a tally, tally, tally, tally, tally, tally-ho !

II.

O ! is it not—O ! is it not—a ſpirit-ſtirring ſound,

The eager notes from tuneful throats that tell a
  fox is found ?
O ! is it not—O ! is it not—a pleaſant ſight to ſee
The chequer'd pack, tan, white, and black, fly
  ſcudding o'er the lea ?

Chorus.

III.

How keen their emulation in the buſtle of the
  burſt,
When ſide by ſide the foremoſt ride, each ſtruggling to be firſt ;
Intent on that ſweet muſic which in front delights
  their ear,
The ſobbing loud of the panting crowd they heed
  not in the rear.

Chorus.

IV.

The field to all is open, whether clad in black or
  red,
O'er rail and gate the feather-weight may thruſt
  his thorough-bred ;
While heavier men, well mounted, though not
  foremoſt in the fray,
If quick to ſtart and ſtout of heart, need not be
  far away.

Chorus.

V.

And fince that joy is incomplete which Beauty
　　fhuns to fhare,
Or maid or bride, if fkill'd to ride, we fondly
　　welcome there;
Where woodland hills our mufic fills and echo
　　fwells the chorus,
Or when we fly with a fcent breaft high, and a
　　galloping fox before us.
　　　　　　　　　　　　　　Chorus.
1868.

Tarporley Song.

1870.

I.

R ECALLING the days of old Bluecap and
　　Barry,
Of Bedford and Glofter, George Heron and Sir
　　Harry,
A bumper to-night the Quæfitum fhall carry,
　　　　　Which nobody can deny.

II.

Tho' his rivals by Meynell on mutton were fed,

When the race o'er the Beacon by Bluecap was
    led,
A hundred good yards was the winner ahead,
            Which nobody can deny.

III.

The gentry of Chefhire, whate'er their degrees,
Stanleys or Egertons, Leycefters or Leghs,
One and all with green ribbons have garter'd
    their knees,
            Which nobody can deny.

IV.

Their breeches were green and their ftockings
    were white,
Tho' oft in queer plight they were tuck'd up at night,
Next morn they were all in their ftirrups upright,
            Which nobody can deny.

V.

Over grafs while the youngfters were fkimming
    the vale,
Down the pavement away went the old ones full
    fail,
Each green collar flapp'd by a powder'd pigtail,
            Which nobody can deny.

VI.

When foxes were flyers and gorfe covers few,
Thofe hounds of Sir Harry, where thickeft it grew,

How they daſh'd into Huxley and huſtled it
  through,
    Which nobody can deny.

VII.

The ſport they began may we ſtill carry on,
And we forty good fellows, who meet at the Swan,
To the green collar ſtick, tho' our breeches are
  gone,
    Which nobody can deny.

VIII.

Still, whether clad in ſhort garments or long,
With a Cotton to ſing us a fox-hunting ſong,
And a Corbet to lead us, we cannot go wrong,
    Which nobody can deny.

A Growl from the Squire of Grumbleton.

I.

I WAS born and bred a Tory,
    And my prejudice is ſtrong,
Young men, bear with me kindly,
    If you think my notions wrong.

II.

I learnt them from my father,
    One whoſe pride it was to ſit,

Ere the ballot-box was thought of,
By the fide of Billy Pitt.

III.

I love the gabled manfion
 By my anceftors uprear'd,
Where the ftranger-gueft is welcome,
And the friend by time endear'd.

IV.

I love the old grey bell-tower,
And its ivy-muffled clock ;
And I love the honeft Parfon
As himfelf he loves his flock.

V.

Frefh youth I feel within me
When a morning fox is found,
And I hear the merry mufic
Through the ringing woods refound.

VI.

And I love, when evening clofes,
And a good day's fport is o'er,
Thrice to pour into the wine-cup
Ruddy port of thirty-four.

VII.

I have told you what I love—now
Let me tell you what I hate—

That accurs'd Succeſſion Duty
On the heir to my eſtate.

VIII.

Old Nelſon to the Frenchman
In a voice of thunder ſpoke,
What would Nelſon ſay to Gladſtone
With his tax on Britiſh oak?

IX.

Hounds I hate which, ſhy of ſtooping,
Muſt be lifted ſtill and caſt,
Like many a fool who follows,
Far too flaſhy and too faſt.

X.

Iron engines which have ſilenc'd
In the barn the threſher's flail;
Iron wires, a modern makeſhift
For the honeſt poſt and rail.

XI.

Knaves and blacklegs, who have elbow'd
From the Turf all honeſt men,
Blaſted names and ruin'd houſes
Fallen ne'er to riſe again.

XII.

Cant and unwhipp'd ſwindlers—
Rant and rivalry of ſect—

M

Pride and working wenches
In filk and fatin deck'd.

XIII.

Song from the green bough banifh'd,
The voicelefs woodlands ftill,
The fparkle of the trout ftream
Foul'd and blacken'd by the mill.

XIV.

A Unionift each craftfman,
A poacher every clown,
Brawl and beerhoufe in the Village,
Luft and ginfhop in the Town.

XV.

Though with all thy faults, dear England,
In my heart I love thee ftill,
Thefe are plague-fpots on thy beauty
Which mine eyes with forrow fill.

The Coverfide Phantom.

I.

ONE morning in November,
    As the village clock ftruck ten
Came trooping to the coverfide
A field of hunting men ;

'Twas neither Quorn nor Pytchley horn
 That ſummon'd our array ;
No ; we who met were a homely ſet,
 In a province far away.

II.

As there we ſtood, converſing,
 Much amazement ſeiz'd the Hunt,
When, ſpick and ſpan, an unknown man
 Rode onwards to the front ;
All whiſper'd, gazing wonderſtruck,
 " Who can the ſtranger be ? "
Forſooth they were, that man and mare,
 A comely ſight to ſee.

III.

The mare a faultleſs cheſtnut
 As was ever ſtrapp'd by groom ;
Nor fault could in the man be found,
 Nor flaw in his coſtume ;
A ſilk cord loop'd the hunting hat,
 The glove's conſummate fit
No creaſe diſturb'd, and burniſh'd bright
 Shone ſtirrup, chain, and bit.

IV.

The rider's ſeat was firm and neat
 As rider's ſeat could be ;
The buckſkin white was button'd tight,
 And knotted at the knee ;

Above the boots' jet polifh
  Was a top of tender ftain,
Nor brown nor white, but a mixture light,
  Of rofe-leaves and champagne.

v.

The heart that waiftcoat buttons up
  Muft be a heart of fteel,
As keen as the keeneft rowel
  On the fpur that decks his heel;
We look'd the ftranger over,
  And we gravely fhook our heads,
And we felt a fad conviction
  He would cut us into fhreds.

vi.

A glance I ftole from my double fole
  To my coat of faded red;
The fcarlet which had once been there
  My countenance o'erfpread;
I blufh'd with fhame—no wonder!
  So completely was the fhine
By the man and mare befide me
  Taken out of me and mine.

vii.

How his portrait, fketch'd for " Baily,"
  Would the fporting world enchant,
By the pen of a Whyte-Melville,
  Or the pencil of a Grant!

An Adonis, ſcarlet-coated !
  A glorious field Apollo,
May we have pluck and the rare good luck,
  When he leads the way, to follow !

VIII.

So intenſe my admiration
  (What I thought I dare not ſay),
But I felt inclin'd in my inmoſt mind,
  To wiſh for a blank day,
Leſt a piece of ſuch rare metal,
  So elaborately gilt,
Should expoſe its poliſh'd ſurface
  To a ſcratch by being ſpilt.

IX.

Sad to think, ſhould ſuch a get-up
  By a downfal come to grief ;
That a pink of ſuch perfeέtion
  Should become a crumpled leaf !
Sad to think this bird of Paradiſe
  Should riſk its plumage bright
By encounter with a bullfinch,
  Or a mudſtain in its flight !

X.

But all that glitters is not gold,
  However bright it ſeem ;
Ere long a ſudden change came o'er
  The ſpirit of my dream ;

No defeat ourfelves awaited
    From the man nor from his mount;
No ground for the difcomfort
    We had felt on his account.

XI.

A fox was found; the ftirring found
    That nerv'd us for the fray—
That hallo burft the bubble,
    And the phantom fcar'd away;
We crofs'd the vale o'er poft and rail,
    Up leaps and downward drops;
But where, oh where, was the cheftnut mare
    And the man with tinted tops?

XII.

He was not with the foremoft,
    As they one and all declare;
Nor was he with the hindmoft,—
    He was neither here nor there;
The laft, they fay, feen of him
    Was in front of the firft fence,
And no one e'er could track the mare,
    Or fpot the rider thence.

XIII.

All turquoife and enamel,
    Like a watch trick'd up for fhow,
Though a pretty thing to look at,
    Far too beautiful to go;

He, the man at whofe appearance
    We had felt ourfelves fo fmall,
Was only the ninth part of one—
    A tailor after all!

XIV.

His own line, when he took it,
    Was by railway ticket ta'en;
Firft-clafs, a rattling gallop,
    As he homeward went by train;
A horfe-box 'for his hunter,
    And a band-box for himfelf,
One was fhunted into hidlands,
    T'other laid upon the fhelf.

XV.

He has not fince been heard of,
    Should we ever fee him more,
He will ftand, the model fox-hunter,
    At Mofes and Son's door;
If not found there, I know not where,
    Unlefs, encas'd in glafs,
Both man and mare in that window flare,
    Which Nicolls lights with gas.

The Ladie of the Castle of Windeck.

TRANSLATED FROM THE GERMAN.

(ADELBERT CHAMISSO.)

I.

"FATED Horſeman! onward ſpeeding,
Hold!—thy panting courſer check;—
Thee the Phantom Stag miſleading,
Hurrieth to the lone Windeck!"

II.

Where two towers, their ſtrength uprearing,
O'er a ruin'd gateway riſe,
There the quarry diſappearing
Vaniſh'd from the Hunter's eyes.

III.

Lone and ſtill!—no echo ſounded;
Blaz'd the ſun in noonday pride;
Deep he drew his breath aſtounded,
And his ſtreaming forehead dried.

IV.

" Precious wine lies hid below, in
Ruin'd cellar here, they ſay;
O! that I, with cup o'erflowing,
Might my ſcorching thirſt allay!"

V.

Scarcely by his parch'd lip fpoken
  Wingèd words the wifh proclaim,
Ere from arch, with ivy broken,
  Forth a fair hand-maiden came.

VI.

Light of ftep, a glorious maiden !
  Robe of fhining white fhe wore ;
With her keys her belt was laden,
  Drinking horn in hand fhe bore.

VII.

Precious wine, from cup o'erflowing,
  With an eager mouth he quaff'd ;
Fire he felt within him glowing,
  As he drain'd the magic draught.

VIII.

Eyes of deep blue, foftly glancing !—
  Flowing locks of golden hue !—
He with clafpèd hands advancing
  'Gan the Maiden's love to fue.

IX.

Fraught with ftrange myfterious meaning,
  Pitying look fhe on him caft ;
Then, her form the ivy fcreening,
  Swiftly, as fhe came, fhe paft.

X.

From that hour enchanted ever,
  Spellbound to the Windeck lone,
From that hour he flumber'd never,
  Reft, and peace, and hope unknown.

XI.

Night and day that ruin'd portal
  Pale and wan he hovers nigh,
Though unlike to living mortal,
  Still without the power to die.

XII.

Once again the maid, appearing,
  After many a year had paft,
Preft his lip with kifs endearing,
  Broke the fpell of life at laft.

The Two Wizards.

GIVE ear, ye who dwell in the Tarporley
  Vale,
While I tell you of Beefton a wonderful tale ;
Where its crag, caftle-crown'd, overhanging the
    fteep,
Noddles down like the head of an old man afleep,
A cavern is fcoop'd, though unfeen by the eye,
In the fide of that rock, where it ftands high and
    dry.

There has dwelt for long ages, and there dwelleth
  ſtill,
A Magician—believe it or not, as you will;
He was there when Earl Blundevill laid the firſt
  ſtone
Of thoſe walls, now with ivy and moſs overgrown;
He was there when King Henry proclaim'd him-
  ſelf Lord,
When he belted his ſon with the Palatine ſword;
He to King Richard gave up this ſtronghold,
Therein to depoſit his jewels and gold ;
He was there when the Puritans mounted the
  ſteep,
And defied the king's troops from its garriſon'd
  keep ;
And there ſtood this Wizard to witneſs the fight,
When Rupert's good ſword put thoſe rebels to
  flight.

For two centuries then it was left to decay,
And its walls, weather-beaten, fell piece-meal
  away,
And his home grew ſo dull when the fighting
  was o'er,
The Wizard declar'd he could live there no more;
Till the thought croſs'd his brain that to cheer
  his lone days
Some playmates the power of his magic might raiſe.

So at funrife one morn ftepping forth from his cell,
He uplifted his wand and he mutter'd a fpell,
Each wave of that wand was feen life to infufe,
And the ftones that it touch'd, all became kan-
     garoos.
He had hung round the walls of his cavern infide
The armour of thofe who had fought there and
     died ;
Transforming thofe plates which long ruft had
     worn thin,
He fitted each beaft with a jacket of fkin ;
Then pluck'd from each fword blade its black
     leather fheath,
Which he twifted and ftuck as a tail underneath.

And there, as a fhepherd fits watching his flock,
Sits this kangaroo keeper a-perch on his rock,
Invifible ftill, but his care night and day
Is to feed them and watch left they wander aftray.
Ever anxious, he guards them more tenderly ftill,
When the huntfman his pack has let loofe on the
     hill ;
And thofe hounds, terror ftricken, all riot efchew,
When they hear a ftrange voice crying, " Ware
     Kangaroo ! "

To this Wizard invifible bidding farewell,
Of another I yet have a ftory to tell ;

No invifible fprite ! when he ftands full in view,
You will own him a man, and a goodly man too.
He it is who by dint of his magical fkill
Uplifted the ftones from the high Stanna hill ;
Nor paus'd till thofe fragments, pil'd up to the fky,
Affum'd the fair form of that caftle hard by ;
He brandifh'd his fpade, and along the hill-fide
The afcent, by a roadway, made eafy and wide ;
Unlike the hid portal I fpoke of before,
Very plain to the eye is his wide open door ;
Where the tiles of the pavement, the ftones of
    the wall
Unceafingly echo a welcome to all.
There are ftables where fteeds ftand by tens in a
    row,
There are chambers above, and vaft cellars below ;
Each bed in thofe chambers holds nightly a gueft,
Each bin in that cellar is fill'd with the beft.

When this Wizard wends forth from his turreted
    walls,
Four horfes are bitted and led from their ftalls,
He mounts and looks down on a team from his
    box,
All perfect in fhape from their heads to their
    hocks ;
The coats that they carry are burnifh'd like gold,
Their fire by a touch of his finger controll'd ;

A whip for his wand, when their paces he fprings,
You might fancy their fhoulders were furnifh'd
　　with wings;
Away! rough or fmooth, whether up hill or down,
Through highway and byeway, through village
　　and town!
With that eafe and that grace with which ladies
　　can wheedle
Stubborn filk through the eye of a delicate needle,
Through the arch with huge portal on either fide
　　hung,
He his leaders can thruft whether reftive or young;
O'er the bridge at Bate's Mill he can twift at full
　　fpeed,
Charioteering—which proves him a Wizard in-
　　deed.

Faint harp-ftrings at night o'er his caftle refound;
Their tone when firft heard by the country-folk
　　round,
They fancied (fo far it furpafs'd human fkill)
That angels were tuning their harps on the hill;
It was ftrung, I knew well, by an angel infide,
The fingers that fwept it were thofe of his bride.

Ofttimes they who deal in thefe magical arts
Bear hatred and malice to man in their hearts;
But to enmity ne'er was this Wizard inclin'd,

A well-difpos'd being to all human kind
To confole the afflicted, the poor to befriend,
Of his magic, is ftill the fole object and end ;
And each cottager's prayer is, that fpells, fuch as thefe
He may long live to work in this Valley of Cheefe.

On a Tame Fox,

A PARLOUR PET AT DALEFORD, THE RESIDENCE OF THE

MASTER OF THE CHESHIRE HOUNDS.

I.

SQUIRE CORBET! at all feafons
A fox is his delight,
A wild one for the morning,
And a tame one for the night ;

II.

For the fox that fcours the country
We a green gorfe cover raife,
But parlour pug lies warm and fnug
In a cover of green baize.

III.

Or in his chair repofing,
Or o'er the faddle bent,
Corbet, wide awake or dozing,
Is never off the fcent.

IV.

He needs no kirtled houſemaid,
    The carpet on the ſtairs
Is duſted by the ſweeping
    Of the bruſh that Reynard wears.

V.

This hunting man's houſekeeper,
    She, without diſtreſs of nerves,
Oft amongſt the currant jelly
    Finds a fox in her preſerves.

VI.

Bones of chicken ever picking,
    This pet, ſo fed and nurs'd,
Though he never gave a gallop,
    He may finiſh with a burſt.

The Mare and her Maſter.

I.

THOUGH my ſight is grown dim, though my
    arm is grown weak,
Grey hairs on my forehead, and lines on my
    cheek;

Though the verdure of youth is now yellow and
    fere,
I feel my heart throb when November draws
    near.

II.

I could pardon the wrongs thou haft done me,
    Old Time !
If thy hand would but help me the ftirrup to
    climb ;
The one pleafure left is to gaze on my mare,
Her with whom I lov'd beft the excitement to
    fhare.

III.

Sound wind and limb, without blemifh or fpeck,
Her rider difabled, her owner a wreck !
Unftripp'd and unfaddled, fhe feems to afk why;
Unfpurr'd and unbooted, I make no reply.

IV.

Remembrance then dwells on each hard-ridden
    run,
On the country we crofs'd, on the laurels we won;
Fleet limbs once extended, now cribb'd in their
    ftall,
They fpeak of paft triumphs, paft gallops recall.

N

V.

I remember, when baulk'd of of our ſtart at the find,
How we ſlipp'd, undiſmay'd, through the rabble
behind ;
No check to befriend us, ſtill tracking the burſt,
Till by dint of ſheer ſwiftneſs the laſt became
firſt.

VI.

And that day I remember, when croſſing the bed
Of a deep rolling river, the pack ſhot ahead ;
How the dandies, though caſ'd in their water-
proof Peals,
Stood aghaſt as we ſtemm'd it, and ſtuck to their
heels.

VII.

How ere Jack with his hammer had riven
the nail,
And unhing'd the park-gate, we have ſkimm'd
the oak pale ;
Over bogs where the hoof of the cocktail ſtuck
faſt,
How her foot without ſinking Camilla-like paſs'd.

VIII.

I remember, though warn'd by the voice of Tom
Rance—
" Have a care of that fence "—how we ventur'd
the chance ;

How we fac'd it and fell—from the depth of the
   drain
How we pick'd ourfelves up, and were with 'em
   again.

IX.

Over meadows of water, through forefts of
   wood,
Over grafs-land or plough, there is nothing like
   blood ;
Whate'er place I coveted, thou, my good
   mare,
Defpite of all hindrances, landed me there.

X.

The deareft of friends I that man muft account,
To whom on her faddle I proffer a mount ;
And that friend fhall confefs that he never yet
   knew,
Till he handled my pet, what a flyer could do.

XI.

Should dealers come down from the Leicefter-
   fhire vale,
And turn with good gold thy own weight in the
   fcale,
Would I fell thee? not I, for a millionaire's purfe!
Through life we are wedded for better for worfe.

XII.

I can feed thee, and pet thee, and finger thy mane,
Though I ne'er throw my leg o'er thy quarters
　　again ;
Gold fhall ne'er purchafe one lock of thy hair,
Death alone fhall bereave the old man of his
　　mare.

　　1871.

Farewell to Tarporley.

I.

TO comrades of the hunting field, tho' fad to
　　fay farewell,
'Tis pleafant ftill on olden days at Tarporley to
　　dwell :
On friends for whom, alive or dead, our love is
　　unimpair'd,
The mirth and the adventure and the fport that
　　we have fhar'd.

II.

The feelings of good fellowfhip which Tarporley
　　unite,
The honour'd names recorded which have made
　　its annals bright,

Old Charley Cholmondeley's portrait and the
    fashion of our clothes,
In the days of padded neckcloths, breeches green
    and silken hose.

III.

The upright form of Delamere, Sir Richard's
    graceful seat,
The brothers three from Dorfold sprung whom
    none of us could beat;
The fun with which Bob Grosvenor enliven'd
    every speech,
The laugh of Charley Wicksted lengthen'd out
    into a screech.

IV.

The classical Quæsitum and the President's hard
    chair,
Each year's succeeding Patroness whose charms
    were toasted there;
The inevitable wrangle which the Farmer's cup
    provokes,
Sir Watkin cracking biscuits, and Sir Harry
    cracking jokes.

V.

The match in which though Adelaide but held a
    second place,
No judge was there to certify that Go-by won
    the race,

The ftakes withheld—the winner told jocofely by
the Hunt,
With nothing elfe to pocket he muft pocket the
affront.

VI.

Earl Wilton ever foremoft amid Leicefterfhire
high flyers,
Coming down from Melton Mowbray to enlighten
Chefhire Squires ;
Belgrave who unbreech'd us, and one fatal
afternoon
Firft cloth'd us to the ankle in the modern
pantaloon.

VII.

The foxes which from Huxley gorfe have led us
many a dance,
Joe Maiden beft of huntfmen, beft of whips old
Tommy Rance ;
That good old foul, John Dixon, and his lengthy
draught of ale,
That mirthful day when "Little Dogs" came
home without a tail.

VIII.

The glory of that gallop which old Oulton Low
fupplied,
The front-rank men of Chefhire charging onward
fide by fide ;

The Baron with his fpurs at work in rear of the
  advance,
When Britain, in the field for once, ran clean
  away from France.

IX.

The find at Brindley cover and at Dorfold Hall
  the kill,
The Breeches left behind us but the brufh before
  us ftill ;
The fox that fkimm'd the Tilfton cream—forget
  we never fhall
The fcore of hunting breeches that were wafh'd
  in that canal.

X.

And that ill-ftarr'd difafter when, unconfcious
  of the leap,
I dropp'd into the water of a marl-pit fix feet
  deep ;
Enough to damp the keeneft—but conceive the
  fearful fight,
When I found that underneath me lay the body
  of Jack White.

XI.

The harmony infus'd into the rhymes which I
  have ftrung,
When firft I heard the " Columbine " by James
  Smith Barry fung ;

While canvas the remembrance of Sir Peter fhall
  prolong,
May the name of his fucceffor be endear'd to you
  in fong.

XII.

The carving of the venifon when it fmok'd upon
  the board,
The twinkling eye of Johnny Glegg, the chaff of
  Charley Ford ;
The opening of the oyfters, and the clofing of the
  eyes
In flumber deep—that balmy fleep which midnight
  cup fupplies.

XIII.

Sir Humphrey and Geof. Shakerley whofe friendfhip never fails,
Tho' long of two opinions which was heavieft in
  the fcales ;
In love of fport as in their weight an even race
  they run,
So here's a health to both of them and years of
  future fun.

XIV.

Old Time, who keeps his own account, however
  well we wear,
Time whifpers " to the old ones you muft add
  another pair,"

May Lafcelles in his chofen home long, long a
   dweller be,
To Philo gorfe a bumper, to Sir Philip three
   times three.

XV.

Young inheritors of hunting, ye who would the
   fport fhould laft,
Think not the chace a huftling race, fit only for
   the faft ;
If fport in modern phrafe muft be fynonymous
   with fpeed,
The good old Englifh animal will fink into a
   weed.

XVI.

Accept the wifh your Laureate leaves behind him
   ere we part,
That wifh fhall find an echo in each Chefhire
   fportfman's heart,
May Time ftill fpare one favour'd pair, tho' other
   creatures fail,
The Swan that floats above us, and the Fox that
   fkims the Vale !

XVII.

The fnobs who haunt the hunting field, and roufe
   the mafter's ire,
The fence of fair appearance mafking lines of
   hidden wire ;

A ftraight fox mobb'd and headed by the laggards
    in the lane,
A good one dug and murder'd, I have feen fuch
    fights with pain.

XVIII.

I never kill'd fave once a hound, I faw him on
    his back
With deep remorfe—he was, of courfe the beft
    one in the pack ;
The thought ofttime has griev'd me with a wild
    fox well away,
That friends right worthy of it fhould have mifs'd
    the lucky day.

XIX.

If e'er my favourite cover unexpeĉtedly was
    blank,
Then filent and difpirited my heart within me
    fank ;
But never till this moment has a tear bedimm'd
    mine eye,
With forrow fuch as now I feel in wifhing you
    Good Bye.

1872.

The Pheasant and the Fox.

A FABLE.

I.

OCTOBER strips the forest, we have pass'd
    the equinox,
It is time to look about us," said the Pheasant
    to the Fox;
" I cannot roost in comfort at this season of the
    year,
The volleys of the battue seem to thunder in my
    ear."

II.

" Time indeed it is," said Reynard, " for the
    fray to be prepar'd,
For open war against us has already been declar'd;
Two cubs, last week, two hopeful cubs, the finest
    out of five,
Within their mother's hearing chopp'd, were
    eaten up alive.

III.

" Within our woodland shelter here, two winter
    seasons through,
You and I have dwelt together in a friendship
    firm and true;

Still, I own it, to my yearning heart one envious
feeling clings,
Cock-pheaſant! what I covet is the privilege of
wings.

IV.

" To you the gift is perilous, in ſafety while you
run,
It is only when upriſing that you tempt the
levell'd gun ;
Would that I could rid you of thoſe wings you
raſhly wear,
And plant upon my back inſtead, a well-propor-
tioned pair.

V.

" Think of *Victory* defeated, as to triumph on ſhe
ſped,
Think of *Boaſter*, terror-ſtricken, as my pinions
I outſpread ;
Think of *Crafty's* baffled cunning, think of *Vul-
pecide's* deſpair,
Think of *Leveller's* amazement, as I mounted in
mid-air !

VI.

" To the Huntſman, when at fault, then I jeer-
ingly would cry,
' Not gone to ground is the fox you found, but
loft in a cloudy ſky ! '

Or, perch'd upon fome tree-top, looking down-
  wards at the group,
And, lifting to one ear a pad, would halloo there,
  ' Who whoop ! ' "

VII.

" Thank you, kindly," faid the Pheafant, " true
  it is that, while I run,
No worthy mark I offer to attract the murderous
  gun ;
But fay, fhould hunger pinch you, could a Phea-
  fant-cock rely
On the abftinence of friendfhip, if he had not
  wings to fly ? "

MORAL.

Self, Self it is that rules us all—when hounds
  begin to race,
To aid a friend in grief would you refign a forward place?
When planted at the brook, o'er which your
  rival's horfe has flown, .
Don't you wifh the rider in it, and the rider's
  luck your own ?

The Stranger's Story.

PART I.—THE BREAKFAST.

FOUR friends, all fcarlet-coated,
  Eager all to join the pack,
At the breakfaft board were feated,
Jem and Jerry, Ned and Jack.

Giant Jem, a ponderous horfeman,
  With a bull-like head and throttle,
O'er each boot a calf expanding,
  Like a cork in foda bottle ;

Still to add Jem never fcrupled,
  When the beef was on his plate,
To the four ftone he quadrupled,
  Many a pound of extra weight.

Jerry, bent on competition,
  Spread his napkin underneath,
But the tongue's untiring motion
  Check'd the action of his teeth.

He told them what he had done
  On his cheftnut and his grey,
And when that tale was ended,
  What he meant to do to-day.

Ned was booted to perfe&ion,
 Better rider there was none,
But jealoufy, when mounted,
 Was the fpur that prick'd him on.

To him the run was wormwood,
 No enjoyment in the burft,
Unlefs he led the gallop,
 And was foremoft of the firft.

Jack, who never faid, like Horner,
 " How good a boy am I,"
Sat liftening at the corner
 Of the table meek and fhy;

No word he fpoke, till queftion'd
 On what horfe he rode to-day?
Then modeftly he anfwer'd,
 " I have nothing but the Bay."

Breakfaft over on they canter,
 Till the covert-fide they reach;
When you hear my ftory ended,
 You will know the worth of each.

PART II.—THE DINNER.

At night again they gather'd
 Round a board of ample fare,

And though myfelf a ftranger gueft,
  They bade me welcome there.

Jem, Jerry, Ned, fwafhbucklers
  You'd have thought by their difcourfe,
Each alternately extolling
  Firft himfelf and then his horfe.

Giant Jem, a road-abider,
  One who feldom rifk'd a fall,
The line the fox had taken,
  He defcrib'd it beft of all.

Told them where he crofs'd the river,
  Told them where he fac'd the hill,
Told them too, and thought it true,
  That he himfelf had feen the kill.

Jerry's tongue ftill fafter prattled
  As the wine-cup wet his lips ;
Had the pack apace thus rattled,
  'Twould have baffled an Eclipfe.

Nought I felt would baffle Jerry,
  From the find until the death,
No rate of fpeed would e'er fucceed
  To put him out of breath.

Ned was far in commendation
  Of himfelf ahead of each,

Still there lurk'd *amari aliquid* ✎
  Beneath his flowers of fpeech.

Still jarr'd fome note difcordant,
  As he blew the trumpet loud,
Still dimm'd the radiant glory
  Of the day fome little cloud.

At each daring deed of horfemanfhip
  Amazement I exprefs;
'Mid fuch mighty men of valour
  Which the mightieft? who could guefs?

Till at length a tell-tale offer
  Set the queftion quite at reft;
Nor could I doubt which, out and out,
  Of the four had feen it beft.

Jack had never faid, like Horner,
  " How good a boy am I,"
But I faw within the corner
  Of his lid a twinkle fly;

When to Jack, though in a whifper,
  Ned was overheard to fay,
" If you'll take four hundred for him,
  You fhall have it for the Bay."

  .

o

The Lovers' Quarrel.

FOR a maid fair and young to the portal was
    led,
For her paftime one morning, a bay thorough-
    bred ;
At once with light ftep to the faddle fhe bounds,
Then away to the crowd which encircled the
    hounds.

'Mid the many who moved in that buftle and
    ftir,
There was one, one whofe heart lay a-bleeding
    for her ;
One who thought, tho' as yet he approach'd not
    her fide,
With what care, if need were, he would guard
    her and guide.

To and fro waves the gorfe as the hounds are
    thrown in,
'Tis a fox, and glad voices the chorus begin ;
That maiden's keen eye, o'er the creft of her
    bay,
Was the firft to detect him when ftealing away.

As fhe fhot through the crowd at the covert-fide
    gate,
" 'Tis the fame gallant fox that outftripp'd us of
    late;
The darling old fox!" fhe exclaimed, with de-
    light,
Then away like a dart to o'ertake the firft flight.

Tho' he took the old line, the old pace was fur-
    pafs'd,
(He will own a good fteed, he who lives to the
    laft,)
Her own fhe prefs'd on without fear, for fhe
    knew
She was mounted on one that would carry her
    through.

She had kept her own place with a feeling of
    pride,
When her ear caught the voice of a youth along-
    fide,
" There's a fence on ahead that no lady fhould
    face,
Turn afide to the left—I will fhow you the
    place."

Women moftly, they fay, love to take their own
    line,

Giving thanks for advice which they mean to
    decline ;
Whether women accept the advice or oppofe it,
Depends, I think, much on the man who be-
    ftows it.

That voice feem'd to fall on her ear like a fpell,
She turn'd, for fhe thought fhe could truft it right
    well ;
To the field on the left they diverted their
    flight—
At that moment the pack took a turn to the
    right.

" Perfevere," faid the youth, " let us gain the
    beechwood,
The old fox will affuredly make his point good ;"
Knowing fcarce what fhe did, fhe ftill prefs'd on
    the bay,
Nor found out till too late, they were both led
    aftray.

Youth and maid they ftood ftill when they reach'd
    the wood-fide,
Forlorn, then, the hope any further to ride ;
In defpair they look round, but no movement
    efpy,
Not a hound to be feen either diftant or nigh.

Both filent there ftood they—indignant the
    maid,
The youth ftung with grief at the part he had
    play'd ;
Still he thought, from the wreck he had made of
    the day,
That fome treafure of hope he might yet bear
    away.

Thus the filence he broke : "Until hunting were
    done
I had hop'd, deareft maid, this avowal to fhun,
Till the feafon were over to practife reftraint,
Nor to vex you till then with a lover's com-
    plaint.

But the moment is come, and the moment I
    feize,
Thofe glances of anger let pity appeafe,
Leave me—leave me no longer in anguifh and
    doubt,
While I live you fhall never again be thrown
    out."

" Is it thus," fhe exclaimed, " that a bride can
    be won ?
Wretched man that you are, you have loft me
    my run !

Farewell! nor the hand of a huntrefs purfue,
When the whip which it grafps is defervedly
    due.''

Though that lover rode home the moft wretched
    of men,
Though that maid vow'd a vow they fhould ne'er
    meet again,
Love laughs at the quarrels of lovers they fay,
When the feafon was o'er, they were married in
    May.

'Tis Sixty Years Since.

YOUR heart is frefh as ever, Ned,
    Although your head be white;
We muft crack another bottle, Ned,
Before we fay good-night;
Our legs acrofs the faddle
Though we fling them never more,
We may reft them on the fender
While we talk our gallops o'er.''

" By you 'tis fomewhat hard, Jack,
Old Grizzle to be called,
You know that head of yours, Jack,
Is altogether bald.
Still I'm good, my jolly fellow,

For another flaſk of port,
In memory of thoſe merry days
When fox-hunting was ſport."

" How ſorely, Ned, our Eton odes
Tormented thoſe who ſcann'd 'em,
The traces were our longs and ſhorts,
Our gradus was the tandem ;
Bob Davis for our tutor,
With that colt—ſtill four years old,
Though ten ſince he was leader,
And ten more ſince he was foal'd.

" Unaw'd by impoſitions,
While the lecture-room we ſhirk'd,
At our little go in hunting
With what diligence we work'd ;
When from Canterbury gateway
We ſpurr'd the Oxford hack,
A ſhilling every mileſtone
Till we reach'd the Biceſter pack ;

" Right welcome there the ſport to ſhare,
Himſelf ſo much enjoyed,
How kindly were we ſhaken
By the hand of old Griff Lloyd ;
How we plunged into the river,
Led and cheer'd by Jerſey's call :

' Come on ! ' he cried, ' the ſtream is wide
And deep enough for all.'

" How intenſe the admiration
Which to Heythrop's Duke we bore,
Riding royally to covert
In his chariot-and-four ;
Cigars, as yet a novelty,
His Grace's ire provoking,
' What chance to pick the ſcent up,
Filthy fellows ! they are ſmoking.'

" The cheer of Philip Payne as he
The echoing woodlands drew,
The ſcarlet coats contending
With the coats of buff and blue ;
Stone walls o'er which without a hitch
The thoroughbred ones flew,
While blown and tir'd the hunter hir'd
Roll'd like a ſpent ball through."

" Well, Jack, do I remember
With what glee we ſallied forth
To the fixtures of Ralph Lambton
When our home was in the North ;
How, when the day was over,
We around the Sedgefield fire,
Sang ' Ballinamoniora '
In honour of the Squire.

" And that week with old Sir Harry
Which at Tarporley we fpent,
Where Chefter's dewy paftures
Are renown'd for holding fcent;
Where Dorfold's Squire o'er faddle flaps
Unpadded threw his leg,
Where ftride for ftride, rode fide by fide,
Sir Richard and John Glegg.

" That Rupert of the hunting-field,
Tom Smith the lion-hearted,
Where grew the fence, where flow'd the ftream,
Could baffle him when ftarted?
A game-cock in the battle ring,
An eagle in his flight,
A fhooting ftar when mounted,
But a fixed one in the fight.

" Where now that manly fcience
Which we witnefs'd in the match,
When Crib by fwarthy Molyneux
Was challeng'd to the fcratch?
Where now thofe ruddy rectors
Who the field fo often led?
Youth needs muft, chafe the fteeple
Since the parfon hides his head."

" Though no longer what we were, Ned,
Ere the reign of good Queen Vic,

Methinks we ſtill could teach them
How their fathers did the trick;
I hold the young ones cheap, Ned——"
" Huſh, your ſon is at the door,
With his pipe of Latakia,
We had better ſay no more."

The Cloſe of the Seaſon.

SPRING! I will give you the reaſon in rhyme
    Why for hunting I hold it the pleaſanteſt
        time,
When the gorſe 'gins to bloſſom, the hazel to
        ſprout,
When Spring flowers and Spring captains together
        come out.

When with ſmiles and with ſunſhine all nature
        looks gay,
When the fair one, equipped in freſh hunting
        array,
No ſplaſh of mud dirt to encumber the ſkirt,
Though no fox ſhould be found, may find leiſure
        to flirt.

When aſſured of ſucceſs, ere the ſteeplechaſe day,
Jones writes to his tailor imploring delay,

When the filk jacket wins he will pay for the
    pink,
Is the promife, when written, worth paper and
    ink ?

November's young fox, as yet timid and fhy,
O'er a country unknown will fcarce venture
    to fly;
One fpared through the winter to wander aftray,
Leads the pack ftoutly back to his home far
    away.

Chill'd by checks and wrong cafts, which the
    fcurry impede,
You may chance in December to lofe a good
    fteed ;
And what rider unvex'd can his temper reftrain,
Urging home a tired hunter through darknefs
    and rain !

Trotting homeward in Spring on the hope we
    rely
That we reach it ere dark with our hunting-coat
    dry ;
The horfe undiftrefs'd by the work he has
    done,
The rider well pleafed with his place in the
    run.

This world, can it fhow fuch a picture of woe
As a frozen-out Mafter imprifon'd in fnow?
His feet on the fender he rides his arm-chair,
Even ' Baily' avails not to foothe his defpair.

Old fteeds there may be, fhowing figns of decay,
Lagging laft in the field where they once led the
        way,
With the glory o'er-burthen'd of gallops bygone,
Lefs of fpring in their action as Spring cometh
        on.

Good fport with good cheer merry Chriftmas
        may bring,
But the joy of all joys is a gallop in Spring,
By the thought, when a brook we encounter
        made bold,
That the ftream is lefs rapid, the water lefs cold.

When each cheer is by fong of fweet birds
        echoed back,
Their mufic a prelude to that of the pack;
When clouds foft and foutherly ftreak the blue
        fky,
When the turf is elaftic and fcent is breaft high.

Pleafure's fweetnefs, fays Moore, is fo flow to
        come forth,
That ne'er till it dies do we know half its worth;

What the joy which firft welcomes the fport
  when begun,
To the keennefs infpired by the feafon's laft run !

POSTSCRIPT.

Exceptions there will be, and Spring, as we know,
On her face will fometimes wear a mafk of
  white fnow,
A note of this fact we may henceforth affix
To March eighteen hundred and feventy-fix.

Such grieves us the more, fince to vifit our
  fhore
And to fhare in our fport, a fair Emprefs came
  o'er;
Still, howe'er chill and cheerlefs our climate
  this year,
Warm hearts are not wanting to welcome her
  here.

Oft again may her prefence our hunting field
  grace,
When Spring more invitingly fmiles on the chafe;
Well indeed in that fport may all England take
  pride,
Which can lure fuch a gueft here a-hunting to
  ride.

Lines

ON READING AN EXTRACT FROM THE HUNTING DIARY OF
VERNON DELVES BROUGHTON, ESQ., SHOWING HOW AND
WHERE THE DUKE OF GRAFTON'S HOUNDS KILLED THEIR
GOOSEHOLME FOX ON 29TH NOVEMBER, 1872.

A FOX, by the pack forely prefs'd in his
flight,
Reaching Marfton St. Lawrence began to take
fright;
In the houfekeeper's room how alarming the
crafh,
As he fhot like a thunderbolt in at the fafh!
They fcreech'd with one voice when he firft came
in view,
But the halloa they gave was a hullaballoo;
Such a duft was ne'er raif'd in that parlour
before
As now raif'd by the brufh which was fweeping
the floor;
Too late the old butler indignantly cried
'Not at home,' the whole pack was already
infide;
Though the houfewife's preferves harbour'd mice
by the fcore,
No fox until now had fet foot in her ftore.

Array'd in her beft, the laft perquifite gown,
Alas ! for the lady's maid, poor Mrs. Brown,
Much diftrefs'd by the worry, the gown which
　　fhe wore
Like the fox torn to pieces ftill worried her
　　more ;
The table o'erturn'd, and the teacups difperf'd,
Such a break-up before never ended a burft ;
The fervants pick'd up broken platter and bowl ;
They call'd ever after that parlour Pug's hole,
And a pad, which next morning was found on
　　the floor,
By the Page as a trophy was nail'd to the door.

Lines

FOR INSCRIPTION ON THE STONE INTENDED TO MARK THE
　　SPOT WHERE THE TWO GENTLEMEN, WHOSE BOAT WAS
　　UPSET ON LOCHQUOICH, WERE FORTUNATELY LANDED.

" Mr. Allfopp and Mr. Burton, of Burton-on-Trent, have
had a narrow efcape from drowning.　On Friday laft they
went out fifhing on Lochquoich, the boat was upfet and
they were thrown into the water.　Clinging to the fide of
the boat they were drifted afhore on M'Phee's Ifland, a
diftance of about 1,000 yards from the fcene of the accident.
They were much exhaufted, and experienced great difficulty
in wading afhore through the heavy furf."

MALT and Hops while here afloat
    Together in a fiſhing-boat,
On which of them to lay the fault
We know not, whether Hops or Malt;
But though oppoſ'd to heavy wet,
Between them they the boat upſet;
Hops and Malt it little ſuited
To be to ſuch extent diluted;
For who would of the brew partake
When moiſten'd by a whole Scotch lake!
Scarce left was any ſpirit more
In either, when they reach'd the ſhore,
Moſt thankful that they both had not
By this diſaſter gone to pot;
The ſtrength which bitter ale ſupplied
The bitterneſs of death defied,
Or they, by water carried here,
Had hence been carried on their *bier.*

Beyond the Tweed on fiſhing bent,
Or brewing on the banks of Trent,
We truſt their boat may like their ale
Henceforth maintain a ſteady *ſail.*

Epitaph

On the Duke of Wellington's Charger, " Copenhagen,"
fo named from the circumftance of his having been foaled
in the year of that battle. He was buried at Strathfieldfaye,
February, 1836.

WITH years o'erburden'd, funk the battle
ſteed ;—
War's funeral honours to his duſt decreed ;
A foal when Cathcart overpower'd the Dane,
And Gambier's fleet defpoil'd the northern main,
'Twas his to tread the Belgian field, and bear
A mightier chief to prouder triumphs there !
Let Strathfieldfaye to wondering patriots tell
How Welleſley wept when " *Copenhagen* " fell.

Epitaph on A. B. C. by X. Y. Z.

I LAID his bones beneath the greenwood
tree,
And wept, like fchoolboy, o'er my A. B. C.

On a Thorn Tree planted over the Grave of " Mifs Miggs," a Brood Mare.

WITH a thorn in her fide the old mare we inter,
Though alive fhe ne'er needed the prick of a fpur.
Six colts and eight fillies the ftock that fhe bred,
Each in turn firft and foremoft the hunting field led.
This thorn if it rival the produce fhe foal'd,
Will be hung in due feafon with apples of gold ;
But whate'er fruit it bear it will not bear a *floe*,
For no thorn fave a *quick* thorn can out of her grow.

The Roebuck at Toft.

AN OLD WAYSIDE INN REMOVED IN 1864.

ON the Mail have I travell'd times many and oft,
Looking out for the fign of the Roebuck at Toft;
Or and gules was the blazonry, party per pale,
The head was attir'd like the haunches and tail,

In his muzzle an olive branch proper was ſtuck,
And the villagers call'd him the bloody-tail'd Buck.

The Cheſtnut-tree well I remember whoſe ſhade
Overhung the bright tints which the Roebuck
    diſplay'd ;
And the bench which invited the weary to reſt,
And mine Hoſt who came out with a mug of his
    beſt !
They have fell'd the old tree, they have ſtopp'd
    the old mail,
And alas ! the old cellar is empty of ale ;
And now from the poſt, where he ſwung high
    and dry,
They have pull'd down the Roebuck—I wiſh I
    knew why—
I dare not inquire at the Jerryſhop near,
Or the man might inſiſt on my taſting his beer.

Charade.

THE Squire, on his Grey,   ·   .
    Has been hunting all day,
So at night let him drown his fatigue in the
    bowl ;
But ere quenching his thirſt,
To get rid of my *firſt*,
    Let him call for my *ſecond* to bring him my
    whole.

Welſh Hunting.

A MOST ſingular freak of a pack of hounds was witneſſed at Pontypridd laſt week. The pack belonged to Mr. George Thomas, Yſtradmynach, and were returning from the hunt, when, on coming into the town, they ran into the ſhop of Mr. Jenkins, grocer, and out again immediately, but with no leſs than ſeven pounds of tallow candles, which they ravenouſly devoured in the ſtreet.—*Court Journal.*

1869.

I.

WHERE Jenkins, in Wales,
  Soap and candles retails,
 The pack, in deſpite of their Whip,
They took up the ſcent,
And away they went,
  Each one with a tallow dip.

II.

With a good ſeven pounds
Theſe hungry hounds,
 Away ! and away ! they go,
While joining the chace
Follow'd Jenkins' beſt pace,
  Shouting "Tallow ! Tallow-Ho ! "

Paraphrase by a Master of Hounds.

Si j'avance fuivez moi; fi je recule
Tuez moi; fi je tombe vengez moi.
HENRI DE LA ROCHEJAQUELEIN.

FOLLOW, when I take the lead;
Pafs me, when I fail in fpeed;
But I pray you, one and all,
Jump not on me when I fall!

Epigram on a hard-riding Youth named Taylor.

TAYLOR by name, but in no other fenfe,
No tailor is he when he faces a fence;
To one Taylor alone can I fitly compare him, he
Reminds me, out hunting, of good Bifhop Jeremy;
For when fences are ftiff, and the field does not
fancy 'em,
Ductor he then may be call'd Dubitantium;
And, when pitch'd from the faddle, he falls on
his crown,
He reminds me again of the Bifhop of Down.

Infcription

I.

STILL, tho' bereft of fpeed,
  Compell'd to carry weight;
Alas! unhappy fteed,
  Death cannot change my fate.

II.

Upon the turf ftill ridden,
  Denied a grave below,
My weary bones forbidden
  The reft that they beftow.

NOTES.

NOTES TO THE HUNTING SONGS.

NOTE 1.

Wells in the faddle is feated.

ELLS was a huntfman of the old fchool, whofe like is feldom feen in thefe degenerate days. He appears to have adopted the maxim of the old Cornifh huntfman— " Mafter finds horfe, and I find neck." He doated upon every hound in his pack, with as much fondnefs as a father feels for his children. In the courfe of his career he fraftured his ribs twice, and broke his collar-bone feven times. After living fix-and-thirty years under different managers of the Bedfordfhire Hounds, during twenty-four of which he hunted them himfelf, he came to Mr. Wickfted, with whom he remained during the eleven years that he hunted the Woore Country. He was then engaged by Sir Thomas Boughey, and died in his fervice, March 30th, 1847.

NOTE 2.

The Vicar, the Squire, or the Major.

The Rev. Henry Tomkinfon, Vicar of Davenham ; the Rev. James Tomkinfon (the Squire of Dorfold) ; and Major (the late Colonel) Tomkinfon of the Willingtons.

NOTE 3.

The Ford they call Charlie.

Charles Ford, Efq., was at that time one of the moſt aĉtive members of the Gorſe Cover Committee.

NOTE 4.

While I've health to go hunting with Charley.

Charles Wickſted, Efq., the hero of this Song, hunted the Woore Country from the year 1825 to the year 1836.

It was ever Mr. Wickſted's chief delight to know that his hounds had afforded a good day's ſport to his friends, though no one enjoyed a run more keenly, or deſcribed one with more enthuſiaſm than himſelf. The "Woore Country" was written in the year 1830, in reply to the following ſong called the "Cheſhire Hunt," of which Mr. Wickſted was the Author.

The Cheſhire Hunt.

SONG.

Come, awake from your ſlumbers, jump out of your bed,
Drink your tea, mount your hack, and away to Well Head;
For who'd be behindhand, or like to be late,
When Sir Harry's fleet pack at the coverſide wait?
                    Derry down, down, &c.

Thoſe ſons of old Bedford, ſo prized by George Heron,
So quick at a caſt, and ſo ready to turn;
If with theſe faſt hounds you would play a good part,
Both the rider and horſe muſt be quick at a ſtart.

Hark! hark! they have found him! who would not rejoice
At the ſoul-ſtirring ſound of old Viĉtor's loud voice?
He's away, I declare! don't you hear? there's a hollow,—
And now we will ſee how the gentlemen follow.

But now let me afk who is thrufting along,
So anxious the firft to get out of the throng?
Who's cramming his mare up yon fteep rotten bank ?
With the rein on her neck, and both fpurs in her flank ?

There's fcarcely a young one, and ne'er an old ftager,
For the firft twenty minutes can live with the Major ; *
Though fuppofing this run for an hour fhould laft,
I hope he won't find he has ftarted too faft.

Who, glued to his faddle, with his horfe feems to fly ?
'Tis a Lancafhire Lord,† who is worth a " Jew's eye ; "
In this run I will wager he'll keep a front feat,
For unlefs his horfe ftops he can never be beat.

With a feat that's fo graceful, a hand that's fo light,
Now racing befide him comes Leicefterfhire White ; ‡
Not yet gone to Melton, he this day for his pleafure,
Condefcends to be rural, and hunt with the Chefhire.

Who's charging that rafper? do tell me, I beg,
With both hands to his bridle, and fwinging his leg ;
On that very long mare, whofe fides are fo flat,
With the head of a buffalo, tail of a rat?

'Tis the gallant Sir Richard,§ a rum one to follow,
Who dearly loves lifting the hounds to a hollow ;
A ftraightforward man who no jealoufy knows,
And forgets all his pains when a hunting he goes.

Then next fnug and quiet, without noife or bother,
On Sheffielder comes, the brave Colonel, his brother ;
He keeps fteadily onward, no obftacle fears,
Like thofe true Britifh heroes, the bold Grenadiers.

---

* Major Tomkinfon.   † The late Earl of Sefton.
‡ John White, Efq.   § Sir Richard Brooke, Bt.

But who to the field is now making his bow ?
'Tis the Squire of Dorfold on famed Harry Gow ;
That preferver of foxes, that friend of the fport,
Though he proves no preferver—of claret and port.

And who's that, may I afk, who in purple is clad,
Riding wide of the pack, and tight holding his pad ?
'Tis a bruifing top-fawyer, and if there's a run,
The Rector of Davenham will fee all the fun.

Now huftling and buftling, and rolling about,
And pufhing his way through the midft of the rout,
Little Ireland * comes on, for a front place he ftrives,
Through rough and through fmooth he his Tilbury drives.

Pray get out of the way ; at the fence why fo tarry ?
Don't you fee down upon us is coming Sir Harry ? †
And if you don't mind, you may perhaps rue the day,
When like Wellington you were upfet by a Grey.

This Grey he can't hold, though his hand is not weak,
And his bit you may fee has a very long cheek ;
But if the firft flight he can't keep in his eye,
To be thereabouts he will gallantly try.

Now, leaving the crowd, our attention we fix
Upon two knowing fportfmen, both riding with fticks ;
The firft fo renowned on the turf, Squire France,
Who on his young Milo will lead them a dance.

The next is John Glegg, and I really don't brag,
When I fay no one better can ride a good nag ;
A good nag when he has one, I mean—by the bye,
Do you know who has got one ? he's wanting to buy.

---

* Ireland Blackburne, Efq.   † Sir Harry Mainwaring, Bt.

Now racing along with the foremoſt you ſee,
Quite determined to go, Charley Ford, on the Pea ;
This moment ecſtatic, this joy of the chace,
His regrets for old Paddy can ſcarcely efface.

For Walmſley on Paddy has juſt now paſt by,
And on him poor Charley has caſt a ſheep's eye ;
But ne'er mind, for no pleaſure's without its alloy,
And ſome day you'll again have a good one, " my boy."

Who's that ? I can't ſee, by " his figure I know, tho',"
It can be no other than Hammond * on Otho ;
If practice makes perfect, he's nothing to fear,
For his nag has been practiſed for many a year.

Going ſtraight to the hounds, never known to caſt wider,
Now comes little Rowley,† the ſteeple-chace rider ;
Harry Brooke his antagoniſt, quiet and ſteady,
And Stanley ‡ who always for buſineſs is ready.

Then there's Squire Harper, whom ſome may call ſlow,
But I've ſeen him ride well when he chooſes to go;
Little Jemmy § comes next, and of danger ſhows ſenſe,
From the back of Surveyor, ſurveying the fence.

But the pride of all Cheſhire, the bold Delamere,
Alas ! I can't ſhow you, for he is not here ;
His collar-bone's broken, don't be in a fright,
His ſpirit's not broken, he'll ſoon be all right.

And now having told you the whole of the field
All Cheſhire men true to no others will yield;
Whilſt the ſparkling bottle is going its rounds
Let us drink to Sir Harry—Will Head and the hounds.

---

* James W. Hammond, Eſq., of Wiſtaſton.
† Rowland Egerton Warburton, Eſq., of Arley.
‡ Hon. W. O. Stanley.
§ James Tomkinſon, Eſq., of Davenham.

NOTE 5.
Our glafs a Quæfitum.

At the Tarporley Hunt meeting, all toafts confidered worthy of the honour are drunk in a " Quæfitum," a name given to the glaffes from the infcription they bear, " Quæ-fitum meritis."

NOTE 6.
Once more a view hollow from old Oulton Lowe !

A gorfe cover belonging to Sir Philip Egerton, formerly in great repute, but which of late years had never held a fox. The Run mentioned in the Song took place on the 16th Feb. 1833.

NOTE 7.
The Willington Mare.

The property of Major Tomkinfon of the Willingtons. She was ftaked during the run and died the next day.

NOTE 8.
To fee the Black Squire how he rode the black mare.

The Rev. James Tomkinfon of Dorfold.

NOTE 9.
The odds are in fighting that Britain beats France.

Mr. Brittain of Chefter. Mr. France of Boftock Hall.

NOTE 10.
Little Ireland kept up like his namefake the Nation.

Mr. Ireland Blackburne of Hale.

NOTE 11.
The Maiden who rides like a man.

Joe Maiden was Huntfman to the Chefhire Hounds, from the year 1832 to 1844. In that capacity, as far as my experience extends, I have never feen his equal. He was moreover as pleafant a companion to ride home with after a run as any gentleman could defire. After continuing in Mr. White's fervice for two years, and after having acted, during the interval, as Hoft of the Bluecap at Sandiway Head, he was engaged in 1846 by Mr. Davenport to undertake the North Staffordfhire Hounds. During the time that he hunted the North Warwickfhire, under Mr. Shaw, he met with the accident which crippled him for the remainder of his life, flipping with one leg into the boiling copper. Suffering more feverely from the effects of this as he advanced in age, he underwent the amputation of his leg in the year 1856. He died on the 20th of October, 1864, aged 69, and was buried at Maer.

So long as this fine old fellow was able to crofs a faddle with his wooden limb, I generally heard from him at the beginning of every hunting feafon, and within two years of the time of his death I received from him the following touching letter :

"Wolftanton,
" Nov. 17, 1862.

" SIR,

" I have taken the liberty of fending you a lift of our hounds. It has been the worft fcenting feafon I ever faw, our beft day was on Friday laft.

" Thefe hounds will be leaving here fhortly to go to Trentham, the feat of the Duke of Sutherland. I don't go with them. I fhall ftop here the winter, and I don't intend going with hounds any more. I have Rheumatic very bad at times and cannot ride to hounds, this being my 54 feafon with Hounds.

" I have a very good entry, and they are all going on well.

" I remain, Sir,
" Your obedient Servt.
" J. MAIDEN."

The following lift will complete the fucceffion of Chefhire huntfmen from the time of Joe Maiden to the prefent day. William Markwell came in 1844, and hunted the pack for ten years. In 1854 came George Whitmore; in 1856, David Edwards; in 1859, Henry Mafon; Peter Collifon, fucceeding in 1860, came into Chefhire on Mr. Baker's refignation of the North Warwickfhire. Leaving in 1869, he was engaged as Huntfman to the York and Ainfley, when John Jones, his firft-whip, was defervedly promoted to fill the vacancy.

NOTE 12.

In the pride of his heart then the Manager cried.

Sir H. Mainwaring, who was Manager of the Chefhire Hounds for a period of 19 years.

NOTE 13.

Come along Little Rowley.

Mr. Egerton-Warburton of Arley.

NOTE 14.

The Baron from Hanover hollowed whoo-whoop.

Baron Often, a Hanoverian, long diftinguifhed as an officer in the Englifh fervice. His hunting accident, and miraculous efcape from a lion in the Eaft Indies, are well known :—

> By the king of the foreft, out hunting one day,
> The Baron was captured and carried away;
> The king in his turn by the hunt was befet,
> Or the *Baron* had been but a *Baron-eat.*

NOTE 15.

Oh! where and oh! where was the Wiftafton fteed?

The property of Mr. Hammond, of Wiftafton.

NOTE 16.
The Ceftrian Cheftnut.

The property of Sir Philip Egerton.

NOTE 17.
Where now is Dollgofh? where the Racer from Da'enham?

" Dollgofh " belonged to Mr. Ford, and the " Racer " to Mr. James Tomkinfon, of Davenham.

NOTE 18.
Save at the Swan.

The Swan is the name of the Inn at which the Hunt Meeting is held.

NOTE 19.
France ten to one.

The Half-bred Stakes at Tarporley had for the ten years previous to 1834, with but two exceptions, been won by Mr. France of Boftock.

NOTE 20.
Brown foreft of Mara! whofe bounds were of yore,
From Kelfborrow's Caftle outftretch'd to the fhore.

" The diftrict extending from the banks of the Merfey to the South boundary of the late Foreft, was defignated as the Foreft of Mara, whilft that of Mondrem ftretched in the direction of Nantwich.

" It appears from Doomfday, that the attention of the Earls of Chefter, in the tafte of the fovereigns of the time, had been directed at that early period to forming chaces for their diverfion. The Earl's Foreft is noticed in feveral inftances, and it likewife appears that it was not only formed of lands then found wafte, but that feveral vills had been afforefted for the exprefs purpofe of adding to its limits."
—ORMEROD's *Hiftory of Chefhire*, vol. ii. p. 50.

Q

NOTE 21.

In right of his bugle and greyhounds to seize.

" The Mafter-Foreﬅerﬁhip of the whole was conferred by Randle I. in the twelfth century, on Ralph de Kingﬂey, to hold the fame by tenure of a horn."—ORMEROD, vol. ii. p. 50.

Amongﬅ the liﬅ of claims aﬀerted by the Maﬅer-Foreﬅer, are the following :—

" And claymeth to have the latter pannage in the faid Forreﬅ, and claymeth to .have windfallen wood   *   *   *

" He claymeth to have all money for agiﬅment of hogs within the faid Foreﬅ   *   *   *

" And as to wayfe, he claymeth to have every wayfe and ﬅray beaﬅ as his own, after proclamation ﬁall be made and not challenged as he manner is."—ORMEROD, vol. ii. p. 52.

NOTE 22.

Whene'er his liege lord chofe a hunting to ride.

" Cheﬁire tradition aﬀerts that the ancient foreﬅers were bound to ufe this horn, and attend in their office with two white greyhounds, whenever the Earl was difpofed to honour the Foreﬅ of Delamere with his prefence in the chace."—ORMEROD, vol. ii. p. 55.

NOTE 23.

It paﬀed from their lips to the mouth of a Done.

The Dones of Utkinton fucceeded the Kingﬂeys as Chief-Foreﬅers. On the termination of this line, in 1715, the Foreﬅerﬁip paﬀed to Richard Arderne, and through him to the Lords Alvanley.

NOTE 24.

Thou Palatine prophet, whofe fame I revere.

Robert Nixon was born in the pariﬁ of Over. " The birth of this individual," fays Ormerod, " has been aﬀigned

to the time of Edward the Fourth, but a fecond ftory alfo
exifts, which refers him to the time of James the Firft ; a
date palpably falfe, as many of the fuppofed prophecies
were to be fulfilled at an antecedent period.

" He is faid to have attracted the Royal notice by fore-
telling in Chefhire the refult of the battle of Bofworth, on
recovering from fudden ftupor with which he was feized
while the battle was fighting in Leicefterfhire, and to have
been fent for to Court fhortly afterwards, where he was
ftarved (or, to ufe his own expreffion, clemmed) to death
through forgetfulnefs, in a manner which he himfelf had
predicted."

NOTE 25.

A foot with two heels and a hand with three thumbs.

Amongft the prophecies of Nixon are the following :—
" There fhall be a miller named Peter,
" With two heels on one foot." * *
" A boy fhall be born with three thumbs on one hand,
" Who fhall hold three Kings' horfes,
" Whilft England is three times won and loft in one day,
" But after this fhall be happy days."
" Twenty hundred horfes fhall want mafters,
" Till their girths rot under their bellies."

NOTE 26.

Here hunted the Scot whom too wife to fhow fight.

King James' diverfion on the foreft of Delamere, when
returning from Scotland, is thus defcribed in Webb's
Itinerary :—

" Making the houfe of Vale Royal four days his royal
court, he folaced himfelf and took pleafing entertainment
in his difports in the foreft.   *   *   *   *   *
And where his Majefty, the day following, had fuch fuccefs-
ful pleafure in the hunting of his own hounds of a ftag

to death, as it pleafed him gracioufly to calculate the hours, and confer with the keepers, and his honourable attendants, of the particular events in that fport, and to queftion them whether they ever faw or heard of the like expedition, and true performance of hounds well hunting. At which his Highnefs Princely contentment we had much caufe to re-joice; and the rather for that the diligence and fervice of Sir John Done had fo profperoufly prepared his Majefty's fports, which he alfo as gracioufly accepted."

Note 27.

Behold in the foil of our foreft once more.

By the act of Parliament for the enclofure of Delamere Foreft, paffed in 1812, one moiety of the whole is allotted to the fhare of the King, to be kept under the direction of the Surveyor General of Woods and Forefts, as a nurfery for timber only.

Note 28.

Where 'twixt the whalebones the widow fat down.

Maria Hollingfworth, a German by birth, the widow of an Englifh foldier. Near two ribs of a whale which ftood on Delamere Foreft, fhe conftructed for herfelf a hut, and refided there during feveral years.

Note 29.

The Spectre Stag.

The fubject of this ballad is taken from a collection of German traditions in French, there entitled, " La Chapelle de la Forêt."

The tale of a foreft phantom, we are told by Sir W. Scott, in the Preface to his tranflation of the Wild Jager, is univerfally believed in Germany. This phantom has often been the fubject of poetry, but the final cataftrophe to the Baron's hunting career, thus defcribed in the legend, I do not recollect to have feen mentioned elfewhere :—

" Voyant le chaffeur noir s'avancer droit à lui, il fonna du cor pour appeler fes gens ; mais il le fit avec une telle force que les veines fe crevèrent ; il tomba mort de fon cheval. Ses defcendans firent bâtir en cet endroit une chapelle où ils fondèrent un bénéfice."

NOTE 30.

" On the flag he would have flaughter'd,
Was his naked body bound."

The ghoft of another *chaffeur*, whofe hiftory is given in the fame colleftion, makes the following confeffion :—

" J'ai fait enchaîner et river fur des cerfs plus de cent des malheureux braconniers, les faifant pourfuivre par mes chiens jufqu'à ce qu'ils tombaffent quelque part, et que le malheureux qu'ils portaient rendit l'âme au milieu des tourmens."

NOTE 31.

A Bedford, a Glofter, to life we reflore.

Bedford, Glofter, Nelfon, and Viftory, were the names of hounds in the Chefhire kennel.

NOTE 32.

Mine be the warfare unfullied with guilt.

" Image of war without its guilt."—SOMERVILE.

NOTE 33.

The Tantivy Trot.

This fong was written in the year 1834, at the requeft of Charles Ford, Efq., for Cracknall, the Coachman of the Birmingham Tantivy, who once drove it at a fitting one hundred and twenty-five miles. Some years after I faw it printed in an article by Nimrod in the New Sporting Magazine, and attributed by him to a young " Cantab."

NOTE 34.

The tent of the Bey.

This tent was brought by Lord Hill from Egypt. It originally belonged to the famous Murad Bey.

NOTE 35.

We've an Eyton could prove to the Switzer.

The prize given by Lord Hill was won by Mifs Eyton.

NOTE 36.

"The Picture of the Chefhire Hunt," purchafed by Wilbraham Egerton, Efq., now hangs in the hall at Tatton.

NOTE 37.

The Breeches.

This cover, once pre-eminent above all the gorfes in the county for the fport it had fhown, belongs to John Tollemache, Efq.

NOTE 38.

Tarwood.

The Run which I have attempted to defcribe took place on the 24th of December, 1845. The Heythrop Hounds were kept by Lord Redefdale. The "Jem" mentioned in the poem is Jem Hill the Huntfman, and Jack Goddard and Charles are the Whips. "The peculiar feature of this run," fays Mr. Whippy, "was the ftoutnefs and intrepidity of the fox. With the exception of juft touching one corner of Boys-Wood at Cokethorpe, he never once fought fhelter in a cover of any defcription. The diftance from point to point is from 15 to 16 miles, and I am fure the diftance run over muft have been at leaft 20 miles. Time, 1 hour and 42 minutes."

NOTE 39.

Tom Rance has got a single oie.

Tom Rance came from Baron Rothfchild to whip-in to the Chefhire in 1830, and remained, through every change of Mafter and Huntfman, for thirty-one years in that capacity, without afpiring to the poft of Huntfman. In the ftation of life in which he was placed, no one ever did his duty better. I have feen him ride the moft unmanageable horfes with rare nerve and temper, ftill keeping his one eye open to detect, and his handy lafh ready to reach any riotous hound. Many a time in the courfe of a run have I been beholden to him for his active affiftance under a difficulty, and there are others, I know, who would, if now alive, gratefully acknowledge his fervices in the field. If after charging a fence you found yourfelf on the other fide planted in a pit (a mifchance by no means unfrequent in Chefhire), Tom Rance was always at hand to pull your horfe out, or if difcomforted by the lofs of a ftirrup-leather, Tom was promptly at your fide to touch his cap and proffer you one of his own.

On retiring from fervice in 1861, the fum of five hundred pounds was raifed and invefted by the Hunt for his benefit.

NOTE 40.

Drink to the land where this Evergreen grows.

" This plant is only to be found in temperate climates. Provence is its boundary to the South, and it reaches neither Sweden nor Ruffia towards the North. Linnæus lamented that he could hardly preferve it alive in a green-houfe; and fo rare is it in many parts of Germany, that Dillenius, their botanift, was in perfect ecftafy when he firft vifited England, and faw our commons covered with the gay flowers of the furze bufh."—PHILLIP's *Sylva Florifera.*

NOTE 41.

This ftrange match, fo haftily made and fo quickly

decided, took place on the Friday of the Tarporley Hunt
week, 1854. The competitors were Thomas Langford
Brooke, of Mere, Efq., and John Sidebottom, of Harewood,
Efq. Davenport Bromley, Efq., was Umpire.

NOTE 42.
" Rolls o'er the cop and hitches on the rail."
" Slides into verfe and hitches in a rhyme."—POPE.

NOTE 43.
Newby Ferry.

The following account of this lamentable hunting accident is from the *Times* newfpaper :—

The lofs of life by the upfetting of a boat in which a
number of gentlemen connected with the York and Ainfty
Hunt were crofling the river Ure, near Ripley, on Thurfday
laft, was fully as great as at firft reported. The number of
perfons drowned was fix. They were—Sir Charles Slingfby,
of Scriven-park, near Knarefborough, the mafter of the
hounds; Mr. E. Lloyd, of Lingcroft, near York ; Mr. Ed-
mund Robinfon, of York ; Mr. William Orvys, the firft
whipper-in ; Mr. James Warriner, gardener at Newby-hall,
the feat of Lady Mary Vyner; and Mr. Chriftopher
Warriner, the fon of the former. The Warriners had the
charge of the boat. The hounds met on Thurfday morning,
at 11 o'clock, at Stainley-houfe, half-way between Harrogate and Ripon. There was a large field, and among the
leading perfonages were Sir Charles Slingfby, who, as already
ftated, was the mafter of the hounds ; Vifcount Downe, of
Danby-lodge; Lord Lafcelles, of Harewood ; Sir George
Wombwell, of Newburgh-park; Captain Vyner, of Newby-
hall ; Mr. Clare Vyner, of Newby-hall ; Mr. E. Lloyd, of
Lingcroft, near York ; Mr. E. Robinfon, of York; Major
Muffinden, Captain Molyneux, the Hon. Henry Molyneux,
Captain Key, of Fulford ; Mr. White, and feveral of the
officers of the 15th Huffars, ftationed at York ; Mr. Wood,

of Bellwood; Mr. William Ingleby, of Ripley Caſtle; and Mr. Darnborough, of Ripon. William Orvys, the firſt whip, was in attendance, and, the weather being fine, anticipations prevailed of good ſport. No fox was found until the hounds reached Monkton Whin, but a good run of about an hour's duration was had towards Copgrove and Newby-hall, and near the latter the fox and the pack croſſed the river Ure. Several of the gentlemen who were in purſuit attempted to croſs the river at a ford ſome diſtance up the ſtream, but Sir Charles Slingſby and a majority of thoſe who were cloſe up made for the ferry, which is almoſt directly oppoſite Newby-hall and ſignalled for the boat to be ſent acroſs. Swollen by the late rains, and to a great extent diverted from its natural channel, the river, at this point ſome fifty or ſixty yards broad, ſwept along with a ſtrong deep current. With little or no heſitation the maſter of the hounds ſprang into the boat, to be piloted acroſs by the Newby-hall gardener and his ſon, and this example was ſo largely followed that in a very ſhort time ſome twelve or fourteen gentlemen, with their horſes, crowded into a veſſel intended to accommodate only half that number. Thoſe who entered the boat were Sir Charles Slingſby, Orvys (the whip), Sir George Wombwell, Captain Vyner, Mr. Clare Vyner, Mr. Lloyd, Mr. Robinſon, Major Muſſinden, Captain Molyneux, the Hon. Henry Molyneux, Captain Key, Mr. White, and ſome more military officers from York Barracks. Viſcount Downe, Lord Laſcelles, and ſeveral others, who were either unable to find room in the boat, or had their doubts as to its ſafety, remained on the banks awaiting its return. No warning voice cautioned them when they ſtarted on what proved to ſome of them a fatal journey; indeed, their apparent luck in having gained the ſtart of the others was looked on with many envious eyes. Any ſuch feeling, was, however, of ſhort duration. Seizing the chain by which the flat-bottomed boat is propelled,

Captain Vyner and his brother pushed it off from the river side, and sent the vessel right into the stream. Before one-third of the distance had been traversed, Sir Charles Slingsby's horse became restive, and kicked the animal belonging to Sir George Wombwell. The latter, a high-mettled chestnut, returned the kick, and something very like a panic arose among the horses. The boat was swayed first to one side and then to the other, and finally it was fairly turned bottom upwards. The scene which then ensued was of a very painful character. For a moment the slimy bottom of the boat, rocked to and fro by the struggling of the men and horses, was all that could be seen by the spectators on the bank; then here and there in different parts of the stream heads began to appear, only to sink again amid agonized cries, and hands and arms were flung up in despair. Horses were seen to battle with the current, striking out regardless of the injuries they inflicted on their masters, who were also swept by the current out of the reach of those anxious to afford relief. In some cases, however, the prompt measures taken by the spectators were effectual. Those who could swim cast off their coats and plunged to save their friends, while others, not so happily gifted, took less vigorous, though not less useful, steps. Lines formed of whips, were tied together, and thrown within reach of the drowning men, and several beams of wood which fortunately lay scattered about, were quickly launched on the stream. Captain Vyner was one of the first to get his head out of water, and to save himself from the current by clinging to the upturned vessel. After a vigorous struggle he reached the top of the boat, and was able to assist first Sir George Wombwell and afterwards one of the York officers to the same position. Mr. White got on shore by means of the chain stretched across the ferry, while others were rescued by the means adopted for their safety from the banks. In a very few minutes, however, it was found that six men and eleven horfes had been drowned. Two horfes were refcued. An account in a local journal fays feveral gentlemen and horfes were under the boat when it floated bottom upwards. Among thele were Sir George Wombwell and an officer from York, who was very badly kicked by the horfes. Sir Charles Slingfby was feen by the fpectators on the bank to ftrike out for the oppofite fhore, but when nearing it he threw up his hands, and the laft feen of him was his body floating down the river with his head and legs under water. None of the others drowned were feen at all. Every effort was made by thofe upon the bank to refcue the fufferers. Mr. William Ingilby threw off his coat and plunged into the river, and made a defperate effort to reach Sir Charles Slingfby, but in this he unhappily failed, and with great difficulty and in a ftate of complete exhauftion reached the fhore. Captain Vyner and Captain Prefton plunged into the river in the hope of rendering affiftance. Mr. Bartram, of Harrogate, rendered very active aid, and fucceeded in affifting to the fhore one of thofe who had been thrown into the river, and had clung to the chain of the ferry. The body of Sir Charles Slingfby was difcovered three hundred yards below the fcene of the accident by Mr. Denifon, of Ripon, and Mr. Wood, of the fame city, about half-paft four o'clock. The bodies of Captain Lloyd and Mr. Robinfon were afterwards taken out of the river, and all were conveyed to Newby-hall to await a coroner's inqueft. Yefterday two more of the bodies were recovered, thofe of William Orvys and Chriftopher Warriner, the eldeft of that name. The only body now to be recovered is that of Chriftopher Warriner's fon. Mr. Robinfon's watch had ftopped at ten minutes to two o'clock. Sir Charles Slingfby was riding one of the oldeft and moft favourite of his hunters, "Old Saltfifh," which was difcovered lying near the mafter whom it had ferved fo faithfully for fome fifteen years.

We need hardly ftate that the intelligence of this melancholy cataftrophe has caft a gloom over the whole diftrict. Sir Charles Slingfby's amiable difpofition and genial manners rendered him moft defervedly popular throughout the whole of the Riding. The deceafed, who was unmarried, was the tenth baronet. He was fon of Charles Slingfby, Efq., who was fecond fon of Sir Thomas Turner Slingfby, eighth baronet. He was born on the 22nd of Auguft, 1824; fucceeded his uncle, Sir Thomas, in February, 1835; entered the Royal Horfe Guards 1843, became Lieutenant 1845, and retired 1847. He was a deputy lieutenant and a magif-trate for the Weft Riding of Yorkfhire. His fifter, Emma Louifa Catherine, who is ftill living, married in 1860 Captain Leflie, of the Royal Horfe Guards. Mr. Robinfon, who had the reputation of being one of the beft riders in the county of York, lived at one time at Thorpegreen-hall, near Oufeburn, which he fold not long ago to Mr. H. S. Thompfon, of Kirby-hall, whofe eftate it adjoins. Orvys had long been connected with the York and Ainfty hounds, and was one of the moft experienced whips in Yorkfhire. Both the Warriners were married. The elder leaves nine children, and the younger a wife and three children.

In confequence of this lamentable occurrence the meets of the York and Ainfty hounds have been fufpended, and that of the Bramham Moor hounds, appointed for yefterday (Friday) did not take place.

Among the gentlemen who were faved after the boat had been upfet were Major Muffinden, Captain Molyneux, the Hon. Henry Molyneux, Mr. White, of the 15th Huffars, ftationed at York; and Captain Key, of Fulford, near York.

HUNTING SONGS.   237

The Field, Feb. 13, 1869.
The fearful Accident with the York and Ainfty.

FROM AN EYE-WITNESS.

It was a beautiful morning on Thurfday, February 4, when the York and Ainfty met at Stainley Houfe. We chopped the firft fox in Cayton Gill, but found again in Monckton Whin at 12.40. There was a fplendid fcent, but the fox twifted about a good deal, and, though the pace was tremendous, yet, after an hour's running, the fox croffed the river at Newby, juft in front of the hounds, and only about two miles and a half from where he was found.

The river was very high from the floods, and a very ftrong ftream was running, in confequence of which the fox was carried over Newby Weir, and the whole of the hounds alfo ; but they all got out fafely, and took up the fcent immediately on the oppofite fide. There is a ford juft below, with pofts marked with different diftances up to the height of five feet, fo as to fhow where the river is fordable ; but on that day the river was fo high that not even the pofts were vifible. We were all, therefore, obliged to make for the ferry.

The ferry boat was overloaded, and no fooner did it get into the ftream than the water began to rufh in over the fides. Sir Charles Slingfby's horfe, Old Saltfifh (whom he bought the firft year he took the hounds, fifteen years ago), finding there was fomething wrong, jumped into the water. Sir Charles held on to the reins, to induce him to fwim alongfide, but, not calculating fufficiently the force of the ftream and the weight of the horfe, he was overbalanced and fell in. (I have feen feveral papers ftate that there was then a rufh made to one fide ; but the horfes were fo clofely packed on board, like bullocks in a bullock truck, that they could not have moved from any caufe.) The boat then fwayed once or twice, and finally turned completely over, for feveral feconds leaving nothing to the view but the bottom of the boat. It feemed impoffible that any fhould be faved, but by degrees heads began to appear; and Mr. Clare Vyner, having fcrambled on to the upturned boat, gallantly affifted all he could reach to gain the fame haven. The boat, being ftill held by the chain, acted as a break-water, and therefore all thofe who came up near the boat had no ftream to contend againft. Unfortunately, Sir Charles Slingfby was fome way down the ftream, in the full force of the current. He ftruggled gamely to reach the boat, but it was hopelefs. If he had only turned and fwum with the ftream, in all human probability he would have been faved; for when he was finally exhaufted he fank (ftill ftruggling to reach the boat) clofe to the north fhore, whither he had been carried by the ftream, but where, unfortunately, there was no one to help. Old Saltfifh followed his mafter like a dog to the very end, and at laft fwam paft him, unfor-tunately with the near fide next to Sir Charles, who with his laft effort tried to grafp the horfe's neck; but the mane being on the oppofite fide, he only fucceeded in catching the bridle. Both immediately fank—Sir Charles never to be feen again alive, but the old horfe rofe again to the fur-face, and then fwam afhore.

Mr. Robinfon—who was always extremely nervous in croffing ferries, as he was unable to fwim, and always enter-tained a horror of being drowned—according to his ufual cuftom, never got off his horfe on entering the boat, and when it upfet he rode feveral yards down ftream, ftill fitting on his horfe. He looked calmly round, as if to choofe the beft landing place, when his horfe fuddenly fank, either from being exhaufted before he came to the top, or from the reins being touched to guide him afhore. After two fearful fhrieks, Mr. Robinfon went down.

Captain Key, being the laft on board, fucceeded in jumping clear of the boat as it turned over, and fortunately,
being carried againft the chain, was able, by making ufe of
it, to reach the fhore in fafety. Sir George Wombwell,
who may confider this as the moft fortunate of his many
narrow efcapes from death, came to the furface on the up-
ftream fide of the boat, againft which he was carried, and
was promptly refcued by Mr. Clare Vyner, though he himfelf was too far gone to make the flighteft effort to fave
himfelf, and was even unaware by what means he was faved.

In the meantime thofe on fhore had promptly done all
in their power. Whips were knotted together; but, as
the river was at leaft eighty yards from bank to bank, and
thofe in the water were more than half-way acrofs, every
endeavour to caft them within reach failed. Every pole
that could be found was thrown, but to no purpofe. Four
ftrong fwimmers tried their beft in vain. One, Mr. Prefton,
of Moreby, had not waited to take off his boots, and it was
with difficulty he was refcued by thofe on fhore. Mr.
Ingilby, of Ripley Caftle, and Captain Vyner, of Linton
Spring, fucceeded in reaching Mr. Lloyd, who was doing
his beft to gain the fouth fhore. They had brought him
almoft in reach of thofe on the bank, when he fuddenly fank;
and they, exhaufted by the long run, the extreme coldnefs
of the water, and the force of the current, were unable to
make another effort to recover him. They were obliged
to receive affiftance from the fhore to fave themfelves.

Mr. Richard Thompfon, of Kirby, fwam off to the help
of Sir Charles; but the latter being carried further away
from him by the current, Mr. Thompfon was obliged to
give up all hope of reaching him, and was himfelf helped
out by getting hold of two whips tied together, one end
being thrown to him from the bank. As foon as he was a
little recovered he ran down the bank and fwam acrofs a
canal to an ifland, where the river makes a bend, in hopes
that the body of Orvis, the huntfman, which was being

carried down by the current, might be waſhed within reach. Unfortunately, Orvis was carried to the other ſhore, and the weir being only fifty yards below, he could make no further effort. The two gardeners were never ſeen alive after the boat was upſet.

Thus Yorkſhire has loſt by this unprecedented cataſtrophe Sir Charles Slingſby, perhaps the beſt gentleman huntſman that has ever lived—one whoſe genial manners and kind diſpoſition endeared him to all who had the good fortune to come in contaᴄt with him; Mr. Robinſon, who was not only the fineſt horſeman and beſt rider to hounds I have ever known, but the leaſt jealous perſon that ever followed hounds over a country; Mr. Lloyd, the beſt man of his weight (he rode fully 16ſt.) that ever croſſed this deep plough—one whom no fence was too ſtrong for; and, laſtly, poor old Orvis, the cheerieſt of huntſmen and the moſt civil of ſervants. Four better-known men, and whoſe loſs would be more deeply mourned for, could not be found anywhere. *Requieſcant in pace.* The days of the York are numbered for the preſent—never, I am afraid, again to equal the laſt few years.

NOTE 44.

The Swell from the Leamington Spa.

Henry Williams, Eſq., commonly known as "Swell Williams." His father, General Williams, lived at Leamington.

NOTE 45.

A ſketch of this ſeat was made for the Author in the year 1833, and the originai then exiſted in the garden of General Moore, at Hampton Court.

CHISWICK PRESS:—C. WHITTINGHAM, TOOKS COURT,
CHANCERY LANE.

www.ingramcontent.com/pod-product-compliance
Lightning Source LLC
Chambersburg PA
CBHW021841070726
47496CB00022B/1800